A Map of the World

(stories)

by Zev Good

About This Book

For Derwood.

And for Bill.

The Sweet By-and-By

The first morning bell rang at 8:20, and the students all filed out of the gym where they gathered every morning. At 8:30, the final bell rang, signaling that class had begun. The man with the gun came at 8:40. The first shot was fired at 8:45.

It was all over the news by 9:30 a.m.

Stephanie, miles away in another county, ran to the phone to call her mother. "Hello?" Her mother's voice was small, distant.

Stephanie hadn't realized she was holding her breath. "Mom...?"

"Yes..." Carole sounded distracted. "I'm watching the news," she said. "Are you?"

"I am," Stephanie told her, and for a long time they both stood in silence, the cold phone between them, and watched the story unfold on their televisions. Finally, Stephanie said, "I panicked. I saw the school and just... panicked. I forgot you wouldn't be there."

Her mother said, "No. No. I'm not there..." Her voice still far away.

On her television, there was chaos. BREAKING NEWS scrolled across the bottom of the screen, followed by SHOTS FIRED AT MIDDLE SCHOOL. The news anchor began to editorialize.

Stephanie heard the words "monster" and "cowardly." She told her mother, "I'm on my way. Are you at home? I'm leaving now."

Her mother lived thirty-six miles west of Knoxville. Stephanie called in to work, got her shift covered, then drove it in less than thirty minutes, the radio off, her mind a blank. She pulled into her mother's driveway and felt genuine surprise to find herself there. She exclaimed out loud, "Oh."

Carole commented on it as well. "That was fast." She didn't seem surprised, though.

"I made good time," Stephanie said, and her mother nodded, then they sat together in Carole's den and watched the news.

At approximately 8:40 a.m., a lone gunman had entered the middle school and opened fire. The school's receptionist had been the one to call police before she managed to escape and hide in her car in the parking lot.

"I'll bet that was Donna," Carole said, more to herself than to her daughter. Turning to Stephanie she said, "You remember Donna Patterson." Stephanie nodded but did not look away from the news. "I hope she's okay," Carole said, her voice just barely above a whisper.

They will sit for hours, glued to Carole's old television set, barely speaking except to utter shock or dismay as the details of the massacre are slowly revealed by harried-looking anchors and dazed reporters standing in front of the scene at the middle school. Initial reports will say it was a student, but those will be quickly corrected and then reported with certainty that the shooter was an adult male. "But whether he was the parent of a student at the school has not been established at this time," explained the anchor, an otherwise pretty young brunette whose face has become distorted by confusion and sympathy.

At times Stephanie must get up and move around and not look at the TV. It is too much to absorb all at once, and so she leaves the house and walks down the driveway where she smokes a cigarette and thinks how lucky she is that this horrific thing did not happen six months ago. Then, her mother would have been the principal and Stephanie would be suffering more than mere shock. She drags deeply on the cigarette and pictures herself waiting to know if Carole was one of the victims, and who the gunman was, and why it had happened. But surely her mother would have survived. Her mother was not a victim, never had been. Her mother had lived through the death of a spouse, raised two children on her own, put them both through college. Her mother had been given a breast cancer diagnosis, then plunged headfirst into a brutal chemotherapy regimen because she would not be defeated. In Stephanie's mind, her mother would have intercepted the gunman at the front door and wrestled the gun from him with her own hands because that is what mothers do: they keep children safe. Her mother especially. She does not allow herself to consider that in a world where a man could walk into a school and open fire on children, a mother—hers or anyone else's—would matter very little. She considers smoking another, but goes back into the house instead.

"Did you pick up the butt?" Carole asked, sniffing loudly at the air. She will not tell Stephanie not to smoke; her daughter is a grown woman now and can do as she pleases. But she will sniff at the air to let Stephanie know that she can smell the cigarette in her hair and clothes and finds it unpleasant.

"Yes," Stephanie said. She fished it from her pocket and disposed of it in the kitchen trash.

Carole has not moved from the sofa in the den. On television, the reporter is saying that the school has been evacuated and they are trying to confirm the number of fatalities. "Those things take ten years to decompose," Carole said without turning.

For just a second, Stephanie was confused. Then she realized her mother was talking about cigarette butts, not dead schoolchildren. "I heard it was, like, two years. Something like that."

Carole shrugged.

The reporter said, "It could be thirty or more."

At one o'clock, the police chief held a press conference. The number of confirmed dead was sixteen, one of them a teacher and another the assailant. The names were being withheld pending notification of kin, which Stephanie found hard to believe in a town as small as Kingston. A total of twenty-one wounded had been transported to area hospitals or airlifted to Knoxville.

Carole sat rigid, her jaw clenched. Stephanie sat beside her and glanced from the television to her mother's face, but she had no idea what to say or if she should say anything at all. When the telephone rang, she went to answer it and Carole stayed where she was.

"How's Mom?" Her older brother, Jason, calling from Atlanta where he worked in a law firm.

"She hasn't said much," Stephanie told him. "I think she may be in shock."

Jason actually scoffed at that notion. "More likely she's thinking how lucky she is she retired when she did."

Stephanie glared at the sound of her brother's voice. "I doubt she's thinking that at all," she said.

"Yeah, well..."

A moment of silence. Stephanie asked him, "Are you watching the news?"

"It's hard not to," he replied. Then, "Man... It's not every day you see your hometown on the news."

"Especially for a school shooting," Stephanie remarked. At the press conference, the police chief spoke of community fortitude and coming together during this crisis. Stephanie thought his words practiced, clichéd, then immediately felt guilty.

9

Someone needed to hear those words, even if she didn't. "Are you coming up?" she asked her brother.

"What for?" he asked.

"To be with Mom," Stephanie answered. She pictured Jason rolling his eyes.

"Does she need me to come up?" he asked. "I mean, you're there. Does she need us both? What would I do?"

"I don't know. I just thought—" What? She'd seen the first report when the story broke and she'd panicked: a live shooter at her mother's school. But her mother had retired six months ago and she'd even told Stephanie she wasn't at the scene. She felt foolish all of a sudden. "I'm here if she needs me."

"Mmm hmm." There was a sound of papers being shuffled on Jason's end. A voice in the background. "Should I talk to Mom?" he asked.

The question caught Stephanie off guard. "Well... Do you want to?"

"If she's fine, I'll call back later," he said. "I just called to see how she was."

"She's fine," Stephanie told him.

"Good," he said.

She hung up and went to smoke again. Her brother annoyed her, he always had. How he could stay so emotionally detached from basically everything happening in the world was beyond

Stephanie. Growing up, he had teased her incessantly about her frequent displays of emotion, and the only time she had seen him express anything other than a calm nonchalance was when their father died. But even then, he hadn't cried; at least, he had not cried in front of Stephanie. He had just walked around, blank-faced and barely speaking, for a month, until one day he was his usual self again, on his way out of the house to go play tennis with friends, while Stephanie continued to feel the loss so acutely she needed a prescription for anxiety.

"What did Jason want?" Carole asked her.

"He just wanted to see how you were doing."

"I'm fine."

"I told him that," Stephanie told her. She looked at the clock on the wall above the TV, a cuckoo clock older than herself or Jason, made to look like a Swiss chalet. The mechanism that worked the bird inside had stopped working years ago, but it still kept time. It is both appropriate and completely out of place at the same time. "Are you hungry?" It is past two o'clock now.

"I had oatmeal this morning," Carole said. She was no longer perched on the edge of the sofa, drinking in the frantic reporting. It was as if knowing how many children had died and how many were wounded had knocked her back, or allowed her to relax. Now she reclined stiffly, her hands in her lap.

"I'm hungry." Stephanie announced it for them both and opened the refrigerator. Maybe she would find the makings of a meal planned before the tragedy at the school, or the remains of last night's dinner.

"I haven't made it to the grocery," her mother called.

In the refrigerator there was water, orange juice, grapefruit juice, apple juice; in the crisper, wilted romaine and shriveled carrots. In the door there was yogurt. Stephanie checked the freezer for frozen dinners. She found ice, ice cream, sorbet. She closed the refrigerator and wondered about her mother's diet. "I can go get us something," she said. "Is the café still open across from the courthouse? What's it called? Stella's?" When she was in high school it was called The Blue Bird, but someone else owned it now.

Carole turned away from the television, finally. "Let's just go to the store," she said. "I need to pick up some things anyway."

On the news, the chief of police was saying they would release the name of the gunman once the family had been notified. "No," he said, "we have not determined a motive at this time."

Stephanie drove and Carole sat quietly, staring out the window and chewing her bottom lip. The middle school was a mile from the house, at the end of a dead-end street which was now blocked off by patrol cars. An officer directed traffic around news vans and ambulances and fire trucks. Stephanie had to go slow as she passed, but really there was nothing to be seen other than the officer waving them through and all the vehicles. Stephanie immediately wished she'd gone another way, but she hadn't really thought about that when they left the house.

Carole craned her neck to see past Stephanie and down the street, but gave up and sat back in the passenger's seat, her jaw clenched tight and her hands forming fists in her lap.

"You okay, Mom?" Stephanie asked her.

"Yes." It came out a croak.

Stephanie decided she would take the other way back, along the river. "I'm sorry," she said, and meant it. "I didn't really think... I forgot we'd pass this way."

Carole shook her head. "No. I'm fine."

She'd said the same thing a lot after their father died, when Jason or Stephanie would find her sitting alone in the dark, staring into space and on the verge of tears, wondering how in the world she was going to make it with two children and a mortgage on an elementary schoolteacher's salary. There had been an insurance policy and it was a nice start, but Carole was thinking long term, and had trouble seeing her way through to an end that would see her children grown and educated and settled into their own adult lives. The sudden death of a spouse had that effect, she supposed, and she spent many sleepless nights at the dining room table, or on the sofa in the den just thinking. "You okay, Mom?" they would ask her when they found her, which they always did because they, too, were having difficulty sleeping and managing the thoughts that never seemed to go away.

"I'm fine," she would lie to them, and smile, and hug them if they wanted it. Stephanie always seemed to want it. Jason, on the cusp of adolescence, acted as if he would rather hug a skunk.

And eventually, she was fine. When or how she got that way, Carole was never sure. There certainly hadn't been a moment where she felt it happen or even became aware that it had happened without her realizing it. She wasn't fine for a long time, then she was fine, and they went on. She made it work on a teacher's pay, then on a principal's pay. Jason left for college—scholarships helped, of course—and Stephanie wanted a car. *Needed* a car, as she would have Carole believe. She was fine. They were all fine. Then they were fine longer than they hadn't been, and that knowledge crept up on Carole, too.

Then came her diagnosis, and suddenly she wasn't fine anymore. But she lied and said she was, even when she lost her hair and had to learn to wear wigs so it didn't look like she was wearing one, she would tell herself she was fine. When Stephanie found her alone in the dark, she would smile and insist she hadn't been crying. "I'm fine." And with the cancer, and the chemotherapy, and the support groups she made it back to fine again without realizing it, and when she did she laughed until she cried and Stephanie found her that way. She didn't ask if Carole was fine then; she just laughed along with her until she, too, was crying.

At the grocery store, they saw Carole the minute she stepped through the door. Stephanie immediately regretted bringing her and considered suggesting they leave, but Carole was oblivious as she inspected melons and apples. Around her people gestured to one another and whispered. "I shouldn't buy a whole cantaloupe," she said, to herself or Stephanie, it wasn't clear. "They always go bad before I eat them." Instead she found plastic containers of cut melon and pineapple and watermelon and inspected those just as closely, doubtful of their freshness despite their appearance.

Stephanie feigned interest in the produce, but she was really only thinking how she would keep the people she saw whispering to one another from moving in and expressing to Carole whatever it was they shared with one another. It was only a matter of time, and Stephanie knew it would be this pity, this concern from these strangers that would shatter the façade of normalcy her mother had constructed around herself.

"What are you thinking?" Carole asked.

For a quick second, Stephanie thought Carole was referring to all the people whispering and what her daughter thought of them. "About what?"

"To eat."

"Oh." Stephanie shrugged. "I don't know. Sandwiches?" It would be quick and easy.

Carole considered it. "Maybe," she said. "Let's see what they have." Like she expected them to have cuts of meat never before seen in a supermarket, Stephanie thought, but kept it to herself.

At the deli counter they chose turkey breast and roast beef, Swiss cheese. "Sliced thin!" Carole called to the woman who would do the slicing. It became a conversation. The woman asked how thin, and Carole explained—thin, but not shaved; she wanted whole slices. The woman showed her a slice and Carole asked for a thinner one. Stephanie positioned the cart behind her mother, at an angle to her own body, creating a barrier between Carole and the men and women who circled closer, concern etched on their faces, in the creases on their foreheads. A pack of sympathetic hyenas.

"That's good," Carole told the woman slicing the meat. "But I'll want the cheese sliced a bit thicker. Can you do that?"

Stephanie was certain the woman was cursing Carole in silence, but she gave a perfectly fake smile and assured Carole that it wasn't a problem at all. "We should have just bought the pre-sliced stuff," she told her mother. "It would have been faster." She hoped the woman operating the slicer didn't hear her.

Carole waved a hand. "Oh, that stuff never tastes good. Not like from the deli."

Stephanie shrugged. She pretended to study the other selections in the meat case.

"Mrs. Spencer?"

Stephanie jerked around at the sound of the voice, someone greeting her mother formally. A young woman close to her own age had stepped up to the deli counter. Stephanie tried to get between this intruder and Carole, but the shopping cart was in the way and she realized she must look foolish scrambling to put herself into such an obviously defensive position, the way a parent might jump in the way of a dog about to maul a child.

Carole turned to the young woman with a smile, a very teacherly expression Stephanie knew very well. "Yes?" she asked the young woman. "How are you today?"

"I'm—I'm fine, I guess," the young woman said, caught slightly off guard by the question "You may not remember me, but you were my principal in middle school. My name's Tonya Tinker... Well, it was then. I'm married now." She nodded to the children in her shopping cart: a baby in the seat, and two toddlers in the basket. Stephanie thought all three could use a bath and a comb.

"Of course I remember you," Carole said. "You had an older sister, too, I believe."

Tonya Tinker nodded. "Yes, ma'am. Carla. She lives in South Carolina now." She seemed genuinely happy to be remembered after so many years. She smiled and showed crooked teeth in various stages of decay.

"Oh, that's nice." Carole acted as if she only just realized there were children in Tonya Tinker's cart. "And who do we have here?" She added what Jason and Stephanie always called her "Teacher Voice" to the half-smile on her face: slightly singsong and just a bit condescending and superior. Stephanie hated the sound of it.

"This is Madison and Kayla," Tonya Tinker said, patting the messy head of each child as she spoke the name. "And this is Ricky, Jr. but we mostly call him 'Buddy.'"

"Such pretty names!" Carole declared. The woman in the deli had sliced the meats and the cheese, and set them atop the meat case. Stephanie took them and thanked her, loudly, so that Carole could hear that their transaction was complete; they could go and avoid what Stephanie knew was coming.

Then Tonya Tinker said, "I guess you saw what happened there today? The middle school?"

"I did," Carole said, nodding. The expression morphed into one of practiced concern now. Stephanie doubted her mother was even aware when she did it, pretending interest. For years, she'd had to meet and talk with so many parents of so many students, complaining of so many things—most of them trivial, no doubt—that it had surely become second nature for Carole to cock her head to the side just so, and furrow her brow like this, and frown at a certain word like that. All to placate irate or genuinely concerned parents.

"I think it's just terrible," Tonya Tinker said. "People are crazy nowadays. I mean, *crazy* with a capital C!"

Carole just nodded. Stephanie glanced around. There were others near, overhearing, wanting to add their own observations.

18

"That never would have happened back when I was there, when you were the principal," Tonya Tinker said. Spots of color bloomed on her cheeks and her eyes were moist.

"Well, we were certainly lucky that it didn't happen," Carole said, and Stephanie thought it sounded idiotic.

Tonya Tinker nodded. "I just don't know what I'd do if it had been the elementary school and it was one of my kids. I just don't know..." Her voice trailed off. She wiped away a single tear as it slid down one cheek.

An elderly man stepped in now. A V.F.W. cap sat crooked on his head. "Have they said who it was?" he asked, as if Carole would have information that no one else had simply because she had been the principal at the school last year.

"I haven't heard," Carole told him.

"Probably some kind of custody battle." Now the woman in the deli has joined the discourse. "Divorce'll make people crazy." She said it with some authority, and Stephanie guessed she was a divorcee herself.

"I'll say!" the old man said, and laughed.

Stephanie leaned in and whispered to Carole, "We should go. We still need to get bread."

"Yes," Carole said, and nodded. "Yes."

Another woman asked Carole, "What do *you* think of this? You were the principal there."

The question infuriated Stephanie, but she said nothing.

Carole chose her words carefully, spoke slowly. "Well... It's terrible. Of course. I'm concerned for the families."

Tonya Tinker said, "I don't know what I'd do if it was one of mine." Stephanie wondered how many times she would declare this. What was the response she was looking for? Might she actually be disappointed it *hadn't* been one of hers?

The man in the V.F.W. hat grunted. "Never would have happened back in my day," he told them all. "America was better back then. Now, though, we've took God out of our schools and we've been overrun with illegal immigrants and it's our children paying the price."

Stephanie glared hard at him. She wanted to tell him that there had been no announcement about the gunman's nationality or immigrant status, but she stayed quiet. This was the typical response from the people of his generation who believed that America was the greatest country in the world despite all evidence to the contrary. People like him would never understand that illegal immigrants were not the ones shooting up elementary schools and movie theaters. Challenging his thinking would do nothing to change his mind.

"We still need bread, Mom," she said, and forced a smile.

"Yes," Carole said again, and to the people gathered she apologized, thanked them for their concern, and moved away with Stephanie.

"There's a candlelight vigil tonight at the First Baptist Church," Tonya Tinker informed them, following along behind Carole as she tried to get away. "I heard it on the news and there's a sign outside the church. Everybody's welcome."

Carole was patient, teacherly again. "I'll certainly consider attending. Thank you for letting me know. And it was so good seeing you again, Tonya, after all these years. Thank you."

In the car, on the way back to her mother's house, Stephanie couldn't stay silent. "God, they were rude," she said, her knuckles white on the steering wheel. "What were they expecting you to tell them? You don't know any more about what happened than they do."

"Well, they were just being nice," Carole told her. "It's a small town. They were concerned."

"But you weren't there, Mom," Stephanie said. "It was just... I don't know... *gratuitous*. Like, completely unnecessary. And that girl who kept saying she doesn't know what she would do if it had been one of her kids." She gave a short, mirthless bark of laughter. "What response was she looking for?"

"Oh, you know how people get," Carole said, using the same appeasing tone and smile she had used with Tonya Tinker.

Stephanie grunted. "Apparently, I don't."

Carole heaved a huge sigh. "I'm their connection to it, I guess." And she shrugged. She didn't understand it any better than Stephanie did. "I was the principal there for, what? Seven years? They see me and they see the school. And there's no one else they can talk to about it, so they talk to me. If for no other reason than to just express what they're feeling about it, I suppose."

Stephanie shook her head. "It was rude, no matter what the reason."

Carole shrugged again. "Maybe. But it made them feel better."

"And how did it make you feel?"

Carole opened her mouth to speak, but the words didn't come. She just shrugged again.

Back at Carole's house, on the news, the killer has been identified as James Earl Robinson of Kingston. The photo shown was a mug shot, which did not surprise Carole or Stephanie. "I think I graduated with him," Stephanie said, more to herself than to her mother.

"Did you know him?" Carole asked.

"Not really. He was quiet, kept to himself a lot."

Stephanie remembered a chubby, pimpled boy with an affinity for cars. He sat beside her in home room and always smelled of Skoal and motor oil. The family had been poor, even by East Tennessee standards, but she didn't recall him being bullied or taunted by more affluent students. They mostly just left him alone. Stephanie couldn't remember ever even speaking to him, but she remembered he went by Jamie. Or was it Jimmy?

"I think he had a younger sister, too," she said. "Do you remember him?"

Carole shook her head. "I don't think I ever taught him," she said. "And he might have gone to middle school at some other school."

They both stared hard at the photo displayed on the TV: James Earl Robinson's scowling face, acne-free now but pockmarked, thick brows growing together above a flat, crooked nose. There was no warmth in the blue eyes, but Stephanie figured she wouldn't be very warm if she were being booked for a crime, either. Still, though, this man had been identified as the killer of fourteen children and one adult, so Stephanie must remind herself that he did not deserve the benefit of the doubt.

On the news, the anchor and the reporter discussed the possible motives for the crime. Stephanie hated when the news did that, instead of waiting for the facts and presenting those; they analyzed what meager information they had and stretched it out over the minutes and hours until new

23

information became available, with the words BREAKING NEWS always prominent in the lower left corner.

"Do we know if any of the victims were this man's own children?" the anchor wanted to know.

"We don't," the reporter, on location, said. "We don't have that information, but the sheriff's department tells us they are not ruling anything out."

Stephanie grunted, disgusted with the reality show tactics. "I'm going outside," she told her mother.

"Don't leave the butt on the ground," Carole reminded her.

Instead of staying at the end of the driveway to smoke, Stephanie walked in the direction of the middle school. She knew it was pointless; they wouldn't let her anywhere near. Still, she was drawn. Tragedy pulled people to itself, people like Tonya Tinker and the old man in the V.F.W. cap, and now Stephanie.

The sun was low in the west, throwing long shadows through the trees as she walked through the neighborhood that was once so familiar to her. All her friends had surely moved away, their parents as well, their houses now occupied by new families with small children, the yards littered with toys. She had played in these houses as a child, slept over as a teenager. Back then—and she realized she sounded like someone from her grandparents' generation—

there had been no school shootings, no children expelled for carrying weapons into school, no need for metal detectors at the entrances. Her greatest concern in middle school had been the reality of growing up: getting her period, growing breasts, the sudden overgrowth of hair on her legs and under her arms. And boys, too, of course.

School had been downright idyllic for her generation, she realized. The enemies were mean teachers, the ones who made you spit your gum out or assigned penalty reading for passing notes in class. Or the popular girls; they didn't have to be the prettiest girls, they just needed to be privileged and wear better clothes and have better hair. Their superiority and condescension were brutal, but it never killed. It had certainly made her feel like she wanted to die a few times, but she lived. Now schools were like minefields: predatory teachers, predatory students, drugs, crazed gunmen. She was suddenly glad that she had made the conscientious decision not to have children. She might never have any.

Stephanie gazed at the houses and wondered if any were home to the victims. Were there mothers inside, pacing frantically, waiting for confirmation of life or death? She felt guilty for trying to peer inside and see, to know, to let the anguish touch her the way it had touched Tonya Tinker. She did not want to be the one who derided others for their response to tragedy, and she reproached herself for how she had acted earlier at the supermarket. Those people had seen Carole and reached out to her, a symbol of the middle school and, maybe, even of strength; Stephanie had acted like a child and, like when she was younger, burned with the shame of it.

She lit another cigarette as she neared the intersection where the police cruisers were gathered to control entry to the middle school. Their lights flashed blue in the settling dusk. From farther away she heard the crackle of voices on two-way radios, saw the flash of red lightbars on fire trucks and ambulances. A crowd of people had gathered on the sidewalk, kept at a distance by a respect for both the law and the dead.

"They took the kids out on buses," she heard one woman say. "About an hour ago."

"On *buses?*" asked another. "Why not ambulances?"

"Not the victims," explained the first woman. "These were the kids they evacuated. They drove them on buses to the high school so their parents can pick them up."

That explained the emptiness of the streets and houses around the school, Stephanie guessed. She wondered what the parents of the dead children were told? Where were they sent?

"I'm just sickened by all this," said the first woman, but she made no move to leave.

"It's all in God's hands now." This from an older black man on the periphery of the group. There were a few muttered *amens*, and Stephanie felt an immediate stab of anger, like earlier in the supermarket. Why did people always invoke God as the explanation or the solution to these things? Seemed to her if God had any control at all, it never would have happened, but saying that would have

26

created a situation she would rather avoid, so she kept her distance and smoked her cigarette.

"Stephanie?"

She turned at the sound of her name, to a man in a baseball cap and sunglasses peering at her from across the street. She peered back, as if that might help her identify him.

"Stephanie Spencer?" the man asked and started toward her. He was tall, built large, dressed like most men his age in a golf shirt and jeans and cross trainers. He smiled as he neared her. "You don't remember me?"

She didn't, but for some reason didn't want to say it. "I'm... not sure." He removed the sunglasses and she recognized him at once. "Craig Jarnigan?"

He laughed. "Yep!"

Stephanie laughed, too, though she didn't know why. "My God, it's been a hundred years!" It sounded stupid, but what else was there to say, really?

"Well, I hope I don't look a hundred years old," Craig said.

"No, no," she said, and they stood regarding one another. "You look good." It was what you were supposed to say to someone you hadn't seen in years, whether it was true or not.

"I don't know about that, but you haven't changed a bit," Craig said.

They had been classmates from kindergarten through fourth grade, then again through middle school. High school, with its more complicated scheduling had split them up except for the required English or math class here and there. He had been her date to the middle school formal, if two kids being driven separately to the school by their parents could really be called a date. In high school, he'd played football and dated more popular girls. Stephanie had gravitated toward debate club, art classes, the fringes of high school society.

"Well, I'm about twice the size I was then," Stephanie told him, and spread her arms so he could see for himself.

"Aren't we all?" Craig asked, and they chuckled, then stood in awkward silence for a long moment. Stephanie searched her brain for something to say, anything. Behind her, a reporter with a cameraman had come to speak to the onlookers.

"How has this tragedy affected you?" she heard the reporter ask.

"Oh, I'm just devastated," was the answer, from one of the elderly women. "Absolutely *devastated.*"

Without knowing she was doing it, Stephanie stepped away from the crowd, from the reporter, the cameraman. She did not want to be asked questions, because she would not be able to give them the answers they wanted.

Craig moved with her, nodded back over his shoulder. "This is some shit, huh?"

Stephanie made a small sound of disgust. "They're like vultures, but they feed off the tragedy," she said. "I mean, we all want answers, but I just don't get the whole victim-by-proxy mentality of some people."

Craig nodded. "I meant the shooting, actually," he said.

She felt like a fool. "Oh."

"I agree, though," he was quick to add, and she wondered if he only said it to make her feel less stupid. "It's horrible, but I wouldn't say I've been personally devastated by it. I'm just concerned about my friends and my sister. I have a niece that was there."

His words did little to assuage Stephanie's shame. "Oh, my God, I'm sorry. I just shot off at the mouth and I didn't think, Craig. Really. Is she...?" And her voice trailed off. How could she word it to make her concern sound genuine now?

"She's fine," he told her, with a forgiving smile. "They evacuated all the students, so my sister's gone over to the high school to pick her up. I'm sure it's a mess over there right now."

Stephanie nodded. "I'm sure," she said. "And I'm glad to hear she's safe."

"Yeah, it was pretty scary there at first, you know? It came on the news and I was at work, and I called my sister and she was freaking out, so I rushed over here, and they had everything blocked off. You know, at first no one knew if the guy was still in there, you know, alive and all... The cops weren't letting anyone near the place, and then the FBI got here... the SWAT team... and—" He stopped, remembering it, his eyes fixed on a point in the air just beyond Stephanie. "It was so strange. There wasn't a sound out here. It was just dead silence."

His choice of the word *dead* sent a chill crawling up Stephanie's spine.

Craig snapped out of it then, actually grinned. He shrugged. "I don't know," he said. "There had to be *some* noise, with all the activity and all. Maybe I was just so scared that's how I choose to remember it: silent."

Stephanie was nodding. "Maybe," she said. "I'd probably be the same way."

Craig glanced back toward the crowd of onlookers speaking to the reporter. Stephanie noticed for the first time that he seemed bald under his baseball cap and she felt a fleeting sadness. He'd always had a thick mop of curly brown hair. In middle school a friend had started calling him "Pubes" and the name had stuck through high school. "They haven't said much else," he said, his voice low.

"They released his name," Stephanie said. "James Earl Robinson."

Craig nodded. "Yeah. I remember him. Did you know him?" He had turned back to her.

"Barely," she said. "I remember he was shy. Didn't have a lot of friends."

"Yeah, you know his dad was the janitor at the elementary school back when we were kids," Craig told her. "I remember some boys used to pick on him about that."

"Kids can be assholes sometimes," she remarked. She kept the rest of her thoughts on the matter to herself, like the possibility of a childhood of being bullied manifesting itself all these years later as a shooting rampage in a school.

He chuckled. "Ain't that the truth?"

"But I wonder what brought this on..."

"Who knows? The world's a crazy place these days, and there are some people that just can't handle it. We can stand here and try to come up with a million reasons why, diagnose him as bi-polar and schizophrenic, with PTSD... then come to find out, it was because he lost his job or something." Craig gave a shrug. "I do think he and his wife were splitting up, though."

Behind her, Stephanie heard the old man tell the reporter, "This never was a problem until we took prayer out of schools." He punctuated his statement with stabs of his finger. "When I was young, we started every day with a prayer and people were just better back then. We got to get back right with God."

Stephanie felt her bile rise. The media always seemed to find the right people to interview in the wake of these tragedies. It was never the level-headed ones who suggested waiting until all the facts were available before commenting, no; it was always the ones who could fan the flames of fear and anger and

31

self-righteousness, who would always blame the government or poor parenting or the treatment of mental illness. No one ever looked into a camera and said, "I don't really have an opinion at this point because I don't have all the facts. I don't think we should guess at a motive." Or, more likely, there were people who said those things and it got edited out. Tact did not scare people, and it was fear that kept people watching a twenty-four hour news cycle.

"Prayers don't stop bullets," Craig commented, more to himself than to Stephanie.

She agreed, but she stayed silent.

"So, how's your mom?" he asked her. "She retired last spring, right?"

"Yeah. I heard the news and came to be with her, make sure she's okay. She knew those kids, I'm sure."

"She doing okay?"

Stephanie nodded. "She's not said a lot, but she's holding up. She's a tough old bird."

That won a laugh from Craig. "That she is. You know, she was my fifth grade teacher."

Stephanie had forgotten. "Are you going to tell me what a bitch she was?" She smiled when she asked it, though. She knew her mother's reputation well and liked to think it was Carole's no-nonsense way of going through every part of her life that had brought her through the death of her husband and the breast cancer.

"Let's just say she was *firm*." They both laughed, then Craig said, "Hey, there's my sister back."

Stephanie followed his gaze to a minivan pulling into one of the driveways up the street. She half expected the reporters and camera crews to rush toward it, but they stayed where they were and the vehicle disappeared into the carport of the house.

Craig said, "So, how long are you here?"

She had to think about that. "I don't know," she told him. "I hadn't really planned to be here at all. I kind of just rushed out of the house when I saw the news."

He fished his wallet out of his back pocket. "Well, let me give you my number. Maybe we can get together and have a drink." He handed her a business card. "My cell number's on there."

Stephanie turned it over in her hand. He was an electrician. She had known that at some point, maybe her mother had told her, but she'd forgotten. "Yeah," she said. "If I stay around I'll give you a call."

"Cool," he said with a smile. "It was good running into you, Stephanie. It's been a long time."

"Yeah, it has. Good to see you, too."

Then he was gone, sprinting across the street in the manner of all former high school jocks who had grown into slightly overweight men but still convinced themselves they were in the same shape they'd been at seventeen.

33

Stephanie stood for another moment there on the street, heard snatches of the onlookers' conversations with the reporter, and had just turned to start walking back when the barricade was opened. "Let's get this!" she heard the reporter say to her cameraman as she repositioned herself in the middle of the street, her back to the opening. "You got it?"

"Ready," said the cameraman.

The reporter's face and tone changed in an instant. "Behind me, you can see the first of the ambulances departing from the scene of today's gruesome carnage at a middle school here in Roane County..."

It was a parade of ambulances, one after another, silent, lights flashing red. Stephanie felt her stomach lurch as she thought of the victims inside. They would go to the hospital and the bodies would be transferred to the morgue where their families would have to identify them.

"God bless them," she heard one of the women remark, then she turned away and started back to her mother's house.

From Carole's, she called in to work to tell them she would not be in the next day. Diane, her manager, gave a hesitant "Okay... When will you be back?" She didn't like Diane.

"Probably Friday," Stephanie said. "I'll know more tomorrow."

On the other end, Diane heaved an enormous sigh of exasperation. On her end, Stephanie rolled her eyes. Like most managers Stephanie had worked for, Diane could never just say okay and move on; she had to make sure anyone who dared call out of a shift felt properly shamed. "Well, I can get your shift covered tonight, Steph, but it's up to you to cover tomorrow."

"I'll call Jess."

"She's out of town," Diane said.

"Well... can you let me know who's not on the schedule tomorrow, so I can call around?" Stephanie asked.

A pause from Diane. "Actually, I'm not in the office right now, Steph, and we're starting to fill up. Call back later, okay?"

Stephanie just hung up without responding. She didn't feel like dealing with Diane's passive-aggressiveness.

Carole was still sitting on the sofa where Stephanie had left her earlier. "You know you don't have to stay with me, Stephanie," she called back over her shoulder. "I'll be fine."

"I know, but... you never know." She caught herself before she told her mother that she fully expected Carole's emotions to catch up with her the minute the names of the victims were released. Every one of those kids had been under Carole's care less than six months ago, and the teacher, too. Her mom was tough, but Stephanie didn't trust that she would

35

be able to remain stoic once the names were called, and she knew the news would wring every ounce of tragedy from the announcement. And Carole had been soaking it all in for hours. Stephanie knew a breakdown was imminent.

"You shouldn't miss work," Carole said.

"I wait tables, mom." Stephanie grabbed a diet Coke from the refrigerator and joined her mother in the living room. "I'm not a brain surgeon. Someone will cover me."

Carole gave a small shrug. "Whatever."

On the news, the words BREAKING NEWS flashed across the bottom of the screen, followed by *First Victims in School Massacre Identified.* Carole leaned forward on the sofa. Stephanie braced herself. She wanted to smoke but did not dare leave the room.

The news anchor said, "We go now *live* to the scene outside Roane Medical Center in Harriman."

There was Kingston's police chief again, his face somber as he spoke to the small crowd of reporters and onlookers. "As we stated earlier today in our investigation, we have withheld release of the names of the victims until first of kin were notified," he said. He did not editorialize, and Stephanie was glad for that. He read the names from a piece of paper.

Stephanie cut surreptitious glances at her mother while the names were announced. Carole sat rigid, silent, her hands knotted together in her lap, the muscles in her jaw working as she ground her teeth with the revelation of each name. Finally she had to ask "Did you know them, Mom?"

Carole nodded. "Yes." It was little more than a whisper. Her eyes were brimming.

And then the police chief was explaining the relationship of the shooter to the victims: James Earl Robinson was the father of one of the students, all of whom were seventh graders and had been in an English class at the time of the shooting. Fourteen of the students, including the gunman's daughter, named Haylee, were pronounced dead at the scene. Seven other students were transported to Fort Sanders Regional Medical Center and were in critical condition. The teacher, identified as Kevin Davis, had died at the scene after first responders arrived. The shooter had committed suicide before police and rescue workers arrived.

"My God..." Stephanie blinked back her own tears. Hearing the names, even though she didn't know them, brought the whole tragedy into clearer focus than it had been all day.

At the news conference, a reporter asked if there was a clear motive, and the police chief answered, without hesitation, that it appeared to stem from a custody dispute between Robinson and his estranged wife, who had filed for divorce and full custody of the children earlier in the month.

"But *why* kill your own child?" Stephanie fairly screamed it, to no one in particular; to the TV, to the world at large. "And why kill other people's children, too? Why should they die because he was pissed off at his wife?"

Carole never looked away from the television. She said, "People respond to things differently. Men, especially. I doubt it's as simple as his wife filing for divorce and him going off the deep end and killing their child to punish her."

"It makes no sense," Stephanie said. She stood and paced.

Carole said, "Killing never does."

On the news, a reporter asked if the gunman had acted alone. The police chief's response was to say there was nothing to make them believe James Earl Robinson had not acted alone. Stephanie rolled her eyes. Reporters asked some really idiotic questions sometimes.

Jason called her mobile phone as Stephanie waited for Carole to get dressed for the candlelight vigil. "How is she?" he asked. "I saw they released the names of the victims."

"She's holding it all in," Stephanie said. "Are you gonna drive up?"

"I already told you, Stephanie. No."

She dragged deeply on her cigarette, exhaled just as hard. "Then why do you keep calling?"

A derisive grunt. "To check on her, perhaps?" Jason asked. "I called the landline but it went to the machine, so I called your cell. Why are you being such a bitch?"

"I'm not being a bitch," Stephanie said. "If I can take off work and come be with Mom, so can you."

"You wait tables, Stephanie," Jason reminded her. "My job's a little more complex. We've got a big case. I can't just run away in the middle of it."

"A convenient excuse," she said.

He laughed. "It's not an excuse, it's the truth."

"Whatever."

Carole emerged from the house then, adjusting the collar of her jacket. She was dressed the way she had dressed as a teacher and principal: dark, somber colors, nothing flashier than pearl studs in her ears. "Is that your brother?" she asked when she saw Stephanie on the phone.

"He wants to talk to you," Stephanie said and handed the phone to her mother.

"Jason?" Carole seemed to cut him off in the middle of whatever he had been saying. "Yes, I'm fine. Absolutely not." She cut her eyes toward Stephanie as she bent to retrieve the butt from her cigarette. "There is absolutely no reason for you to come here. I am *fine*." She added extra emphasis to the word this time. "Well, yes, of course it's horrific. I knew those children and the teacher. I might even have known the killer. I've taught most of the people under the age of forty-five in this town." She paused, listening. "I understand completely. It would be foolish for you to leave in the middle of a pending case." Another pause. "Well, we're on our way to a candlelight vigil. I think it's being held at the First Baptist Church. You know the one, there on the corner. Yes, that one."

Stephanie walked past Carole toward the driver's door of her car. She dropped the crumpled filter into an empty diet Coke can she had in the cup rest and wondered if maybe they shouldn't take her mother's car. The last thing she wanted to listen to on the drive into town was Carole complaining about the smell of cigarettes in her car.

"I'll call you tomorrow," Carole was saying to Jason. "Well, you call me, then. Fine. Goodbye. I love you. Goodbye." She held the phone out to her daughter with a scowl. "It's really not necessary for you to try to guilt him into driving up, Stephanie. He's in the middle of a case."

Stephanie rolled her eyes. She would not remind her mother that she always defended Jason, no matter what the argument was. "I just thought he might want to be here," she said.

"Well, he does want to be here, but he can't." Carole shrugged. "So, there's nothing to do."

"Fine," Stephanie said. Then, "Let's take your car. Mine smells like cigarette smoke."

The face her mother made was only barely perceptible in the steadily darkening dusk. "Yes,"

Carole said, and fished her keys from her purse. "You can drive, though."

The First Baptist Church dominated one corner at the intersection of Kentucky Street and Cumberland Street. Stephanie had to park at the high school and they walked, part of a slow moving, somber crowd in the direction of the church.

Inside, there were no more seats. "I guess we'll just stand," Carole said, and shuffled to the left out of the way of other people walking in.

"We should have come earlier," Stephanie muttered, more to herself than to her mother. The size of the crowd irritated her, for some reason she could not immediately identify. It should have filled her with a sense of community and belonging, of being a part of something that did not take herself— anyone's self, really—into account, but it just left her feeling irritated. This was not a church packed to the rafters with people who had lost someone in the massacre; no, these people were tragedy groupies, she told herself, as she watched them snapping photos with their cell phones, some even taking selfies. She knew the photos would be spread across all social media platforms within seconds, proclaiming their shock, their pain, their utter devastation in the wake of the tragedy, but look! See how they have come together with other people in the tight-knit community to display their solidarity in the face of this horror! See how they suffer just as much as if they had lost someone! She wondered what the appropriate hashtag for the gathering was, because surely that had been agreed upon even before the vigil was scheduled and announced.

She must have made some sound of disgust because her mother turned to her and asked, "Are you okay?"

Stephanie lied without even thinking. "I don't like crowds. It's really crowded in here." She wanted a cigarette. Or some other excuse to leave.

"It's not so bad," Carole said. And really, it wasn't. There was ample space to move, there just wasn't any place to sit.

"Someone should offer you their seat," Stephanie remarked.

Carole was genuinely stunned by the comment. "What? No. That's ridiculous."

"You taught these kids and you knew the teacher," Stephanie explained. "They should make room for you." She wasn't just saying it, either; she did think someone should have recognized Carole by now and offered her their seat or taken her to a seat reserved for faculty. She also thought it would be easier for her to slip outside and smoke, instead of having to endure the vigil, which she wanted nothing to do with all of a sudden.

Carole scoffed. "You make it sound like I'm some kind of... celebrity, or something."

"No, just the former principal of the school," Stephanie said. "That should count for something."

"It doesn't make me special."

"No, but it does put you closer to the victims than the majority of the people here."

They were whispering, but Stephanie was sure they could be heard by the people gathered closest to them and she really didn't care. Let them hear, and if no one among them would give up their seat for Carole then it just proved the point she had made to herself upon entering: they were here more for themselves and not the victims.

"I'll just stand," Carole said. "I don't mind. Really."

Stephanie grunted. "Fine."

More people entered behind them and she heard several more declarations of surprise at the size of the crowd. One young couple decided to just go back home, and Stephanie couldn't help but notice how neither sounded that disappointed at being unable to participate in the vigil. She would have loved to leave with them, and seriously considered telling her mother that she would be back when the vigil was over. She would wait across the street, and be able to smoke; Carole wouldn't even miss her. She worked it all out in her mind.

A hand on her shoulder interrupted her thoughts and she turned to find Craig Jarnigan there, smiling only slightly. "I see you didn't have much luck, either," he said. He was not wearing the ball cap from earlier and she saw that he had, in fact, lost most of his hair. The sight of his scalp, pink and smooth, through the sparse growth reminded her of Easter chicks and only added to her sinking mood.

"We just got here," Stephanie said.

Craig glanced around her to speak to Carole. "Hi, Mrs. Spencer."

Carole smiled and nodded. "Hello," she said. It was clear to Stephanie that her mother had absolutely no idea who was speaking to her.

Stephanie jumped to both their rescue. "Mom, you remember Craig Jarnigan? He was my date to the middle school prom."

"And I was in your class in fifth grade," Craig added. "That was back in, like, 1990."

Recognition finally sparked in Carole's eyes. "Of course!" she cried. "You have a younger sister, too. Cynthia, was it?"

Craig nodded.

Stephanie told her mother, "Craig's niece is a student at the middle school. She was there today."

For a second, Carole was aghast, but Craig was quick to explain. "She's fine, though. She was evacuated with the other kids to the high school."

"Oh, thank God," Carole said, practically panted it.

"Yeah. It was scary there at first," Craig said.

Carole was glancing around. "Is your sister here? With your niece?"

"No, ma'am," Craig told her. "They stayed at home."

"Well, that's understandable," Carole said.

They fell silent as a stout woman in a sweatshirt with **#PrayForKingston** stenciled on it came up the aisle, distributing candles and directing people. "You can't stand in the aisle," she said, loudly but not rudely. "I'm really sorry, but you can't. We need to clear the aisle."

"But where do we go?" someone asked, and several other people seconded it.

"We'll extend the vigil out the doors and onto the sidewalk," explained the woman, still loud enough that everyone could hear and understand. "I'm sorry, but it is against code to have people standing in the aisle like this. I'm really sorry."

Craig gave Stephanie a smile and an arched brow. "I guess that means us," he said.

Suddenly, Stephanie did not want to be there, if she ever really had to begin with. She turned to Carole. "It's okay if you want to just go home," she said.

But Carole shook her head. "No. I need to be here." She did not specify whether for herself or for the community. "I don't mind standing outside."

The woman in the hashtagged sweatshirt stood sentry as the crowded moved reluctantly outside. "Thank you all," she said, and smiled so that people would see she didn't want to make them do this but she had to. "Thank you for understanding." She caught sight of Carole then and called out: "Mrs. Spencer?" She held up one hand, waved as if she were standing on the other side of the church and must make herself seen.

"Yes?" Carole tried to stop, but the movement of the crowd forced her to keep going.

The woman stepped in, effectively halted the stream of people back out of the nave, and gently pulled Carole out of the stream of bodies. "Come with me," the lady said, and smiled. "I have a seat for you right up front."

Carole shook her head. "Oh, I don't think that's necessary, really." She glanced back at Stephanie where she stood with Craig, just outside the doors where the press of people spread and flowed more easily. "And my daughter is with me."

The woman frowned, and Stephanie knew she was about to say how she was sorry, but there was only room for Carole. "It's fine, Mom," she said, more to the woman than to Carole. "I'll stand outside. It's not a problem."

Carole seemed torn, but the woman was smiling. "I don't want to seem disrespectful," she said. "I'd hate to take up a spot meant for a family member, or..." Her voice trailed off.

"Go, Mom. I'll be fine. I'll stand with Craig." Carole relented at last and allowed herself to be led away. Stephanie turned to Craig and heaved a huge sigh. "I need a cigarette, too."

He chuckled. "Worked out good for you then."

They were handed candles with paper disks attached to catch the dripping wax, then moved across the street so that Stephanie could smoke. "You want one?" she asked Craig, and he shook his head.

"I quit about three years ago," he told her.

"Lucky you," she muttered through a deep drag. "I've tried everything but having my hands cut off. What did you use?"

"My dad died of lung cancer." He shrugged. "I figured it was time to quit."

Stephanie felt like a fool. Again. "Sorry... I didn't meant to sound so flippant."

"You didn't know, so there's no need to apologize."

From inside the church, the organ started playing. Stephanie was surprised to recognize the hymn: "What A Friend We Have In Jesus." She hadn't stepped a foot in a church in over twelve years, and even then it had been for a wedding. Craig scuffed the sidewalk with the toe of his shoe, fiddled with his candle. "I hope it's not a very long vigil," he said, and held up the candle, which seemed rather small.

47

"Maybe they burn longer than normal candles?" Stephanie wondered. What the hell did she know?

Craig shrugged. "Maybe." He glanced toward the open doors of the church. "That was nice of them to take your mom up front."

"Yes, it was." Stephanie had a feeling Craig knew she had taken advantage of it to get away and smoke. She wondered what he thought of her for it.

"I don't even know why I'm here," he said, turning back to Stephanie. "Dumb, huh?"

"No," she said, then leaned in and whispered, "I don't really want to be here myself. I just felt that it was important for Mom to come, so I came with her." She searched her mind for a way to explain it better. "I feel like I'm trespassing."

Craig was nodding, but Stephanie didn't think he'd heard her. "I just heard they were doing it and I came." He cocked his head to indicate the crowd. "I suppose they all did. Because what else can you do when fourteen kids get gunned down by a psychopath who wanted to make his wife feel bad for divorcing him?" He gave a small, derisive snort. "Can't kill him, he took care of that himself. Can't bring the kids back... can't keep it from happening in the first place. Too late for all that. So here we are, wondering why we're here."

"I guess it helps people," she heard herself saying, and called herself a hypocrite with her next thought. She didn't think it helped people; she

48

thought it was a way for people to play victim and wallow in a misery that wasn't rightfully theirs.

"Maybe," Craig said. He fiddled with his candle, its flimsy paper guard. He seemed unsure of it.

From inside the church came the first strains of another hymn Stephanie was surprised that she recognized. "The Sweet By-and-By." In a slow wave, people began lighting their candles. Stephanie lit her own, then Craig's. The organ got louder, then people started humming along. Then they were singing.

There's a land that is fairer than day,

And by faith we can see it afar;

For the Father waits over the way

To prepare us a dwelling place there.

Stephanie still knew the words, though she wasn't sure where or when she had learned them. So she sang, not loudly; more a mumble. She had never really been a singer, outside of drunken karaoke sessions throughout college and into her adult life. She did not wish to make a fool of herself, so she sang in a whisper. Craig stayed silent, eyeing the flame and the dripping wax of his candle. Around them, the voices got louder, more unabashed as they reached the chorus which everyone knew.

In the sweet by-and-by,

We shall meet on that beautiful shore;

In the sweet by-and-by,

We shall meet on that beautiful shore.

Then something happened inside her and Stephanie began to cry. Slowly at first, like her singing, but as the chorus of voices around her completed the second verse—"...*And our spirits shall sorrow no more, not a sigh for the blessing of rest...*"—she sobbed, great heaving moans that she could only silence by covering her mouth and clenching her jaw, biting down hard on the sobs. Craig slipped an arm around her shoulders and pulled her toward him, to comfort her, she knew, but it only served to make her cry harder. She hung her head in shame, could not bear to see any face that might be turned toward her with the same scorn she had shown toward Tonya Tinker at the supermarket.

Did they know she was a hypocrite? What did Craig think of her tears? He was holding her to comfort her, yes, but what did he think of her show of emotion only moments after she had told him she didn't even know why she was there, she had only come for her mother?

Stephanie thought she heard sniffling, other people crying as their emotions overwhelmed them.

"It's okay," Craig said, and gave her shoulders a small squeeze.

"I'm sorry," she whispered, and her voice quavered.

"Don't be sorry. It's okay."

She cut a quick glance at him through her hair. It hung in front of her downturned face like the shroud of a penitent, and she was glad for its stupid length and thickness for perhaps the only time in her life. He held his chin high, his gaze directed toward the open doors of the church and the stream of tiny, flickering flames streaming from them. Stephanie saw that his cheeks were wet with tears. *The silent tears of a man*, she thought, and cried again.

Later, they waited for Carole and did not speak. People passed them in silence, without even regarding them, each person alone with his or her own grief. Stephanie saw men, women, and children, some still clutching the burned out stubs of their candles in their hands. Craig had pitched his into a garbage can once the vigil ended, after the singing of more hymns and the naming of each and every victim. Stephanie had known none of them, but with each name read, she imagined their faces and now felt their loss as acutely as if she had lost a child of her own. She felt empty now, thanks to all the crying she had been unable to control throughout the vigil, and exhausted.

"Maybe she got caught up talking to people," Craig suggested, meaning Carole.

Stephanie nodded. "Yeah, we got stopped at the store today. People mobbing her." She no longer resented the notion, she realized. Kingston was a small town and there weren't the distractions of larger cities here, and she had a clearer understanding of how such a horrible thing as the violent deaths of fourteen children and their teacher could affect an entire community. She was affected by it herself now, though she had fought it. Again, she was reminded just what a strong woman her mother was. Carole seemed born to weather situations like these, while Stephanie either scoffed in the face of suffering like a teenager, or she collapsed under its weight, the way she had done just now. Craig must think her a lunatic.

"I think I see her," he said, craning his neck.

Carole stood just outside the door, framed between the church's white columns, searching.

Stephanie waved to her. "Over here! Mom!"

Carole's relief was apparent even from twenty feet away, and Stephanie noticed the slump of her shoulders as she walked toward them. "Thank you," she said to Craig when she had joined them. At his confused look, she went on: "For staying with Stephanie during the vigil. I really had no idea I would be seated at the front like that."

Stephanie couldn't tell if her mother was upset about it; the look on her face was one of simple exhaustion. "You okay?" she asked.

Carole nodded. "I just want to go home, I think."

"Of course." Stephanie told Craig that she would call him and they started back along Cumberland Street toward the high school, the crowd around them thinning the further they got from the church. Neither spoke, not when they got into the car, not even on the ride back to Carole's house.

"It's getting late," her mother said as she unlocked the door and they stepped into the kitchen.

"I might as well stay the night, I guess," Stephanie said. "If that's okay...?"

Carole shrugged. "If you want to." She took her jacket off and walked with it through the dining room. Stephanie switched lights on and felt suddenly unwelcome. She tried to recall the last time her mother had responded so noncommittally to her about something and could not recall. Carole Spencer had always given a clear, firm answer. *Yes, you may stay the night* or *No, not tonight*. And there was always a reason. Maybe she should have phrased it more as a question, instead of basically inviting herself?

"Are you hungry?" Stephanie called out to her mother. "We have plenty of stuff for sandwiches."

"I'm not," came Carole's voice from the direction of the stairs. "I'm going to take a bath."

Stephanie listened as her mother's footsteps went up the stairs and across the second floor, then the water running as Carole ran her bath. She stood in the kitchen, perplexed but not exactly sure how she got that way. She sensed a shift, but could not identify it or locate it. Upstairs, the water filled Carole's enormous garden tub.

In the kitchen, Stephanie opened cabinets, stared hard at the dishes stacked there, at the boxes and cans of food, the Centrum Silver, the Metamucil. She opened the refrigerator and stared at the sandwich fixings they had bought earlier (it seemed so long ago now, had it only been this afternoon?), at a single orange sitting in all the whiteness of the refrigerator's interior. She recalled her grandmother would call it "the icebox," and that had always tickled her when she was a little girl.

She pulled everything out and very meticulously made a sandwich, then didn't eat it. Upstairs, the water had stopped. She cocked her head and listened, but heard only the buzz of a silent house. For a brief moment, she considered going upstairs to check on her mother but figured she would only get more of the distant nonchalance her mother had displayed since leaving the vigil, which would only increase her concern and the strange feeling that she couldn't even name.

She left the sandwich on the counter and went into the den, where she turned the TV on and saw more about the shooting. Now that the victims and the perpetrator had been named, the reports had turned to analysis. In much the same way commentators could spend three hours analyzing a ninety-minute-long football game, the news has called in specialists in various fields to dissect the events of the day and discuss their meaning, as if the meaning was not clear: a man, pissed off that his wife had filed for a divorce, had taken a rifle, gone to his daughter's school, found her classroom, and shot her dead along with thirteen of her classmates and the teacher. Stephanie saw no need for analysis, yet here it was.

"But why filicide?" asked one so-called expert, a woman with no makeup and flyaway hair. "Why kill your own *child?* It just defies explanation."

"I think it's obvious why," said another of the talking heads. "He wanted to hurt his wife. I'd say he succeeded."

With a grunt of disgust, Stephanie aimed the remote at the television and turned it off. She sat, listening to the silence again. Maybe she shouldn't stay, maybe that was what Carole was trying to tell her without coming out and actually saying the words, because she didn't want to hurt Stephanie's feelings. Maybe that was the shift she was feeling, though her next thought was *Have I ever had that kind of connection with Mom, though?* She didn't think she'd ever been so emotionally connected to her mother that she could sense what Carole was actually feeling and not saying. Not even during her father's drawn out illness or after his death; not during her mother's battle with breast cancer, either. She knew women who claimed such a connection with their own mothers, and she had always been quick to envy them, but now she wondered if they weren't simply spouting the drivel they'd heard on talk shows or social media.

Stephanie had no idea what Carole was feeling or thinking right now, and she strained her ears to catch some sound—crying? What? All she could hear was that relentless sotto voce buzz of electricity and, fainter, the sound of crickets and tree

55

frogs from outside, and that made her want to go smoke.

She took one cigarette from the pack, then reconsidered and took a second one. There were six more when she checked, and she was sure she had another pack in her car. The anxiety she always felt when she thought she might run out of cigarettes was proof to Stephanie that she was addicted, and she always considered quitting, then changed her mind. She could always quit later. Craig had quit, and she wondered if she'd need the same kind of inspiration he'd had. And as she lit her cigarette at the end of Carole's driveway, she realized she'd already been given that inspiration twice: first her father and then her mother, with only one surviving cancer. Neither were lung cancer, but didn't that mean she was more at risk?

She thought about it as she smoked. And she considered calling Craig. Was it too late? He may have to work early and be in bed already; people in places like Kingston tended to go to bed early. Or maybe he was a night owl, like herself. She figured she probably wouldn't stay up late tonight, though, not after everything she'd dealt with today.

Or maybe she should call Jason again, tell him how their mother was acting after the vigil. Stephanie knew he would be awake, especially if he was working on a case. She fished her phone out of her pocket, then put it back. She didn't want to talk to Jason. All he'd do is piss her off, or—at this point in her day—make her cry.

She smoked her cigarette and listened to the crickets and thought about dead schoolchildren. She imagined James Earl Robinson's daughter glancing up as the door to her classroom opened and what she must have thought in those last seconds of her life. Had she been pleasantly surprised to see her father walk into the room, or had she immediately known something wasn't right? Had he walked in with the gun raised, sending the students and their teacher into a panic? Were words exchanged, or did he just raise the gun and shoot his daughter, then start picking the other students off one by one?

Surprisingly, none of these thoughts made her cry. Not even a tear, and especially not the way she had broken down at the vigil earlier, hearing those hymns. *Weird*, was all she thought about it, then she lit her second cigarette and glanced back toward the house just as the light in her mother's room upstairs went off. Maybe she wouldn't stay the night, after all. She didn't like the feeling that she was trespassing, and that's how she'd felt since leaving the church. Carole would never say as much outright, but Stephanie could tell her mother would rather just be alone. She got that way herself sometimes. Didn't everyone?

She ground out the cigarette and collected both butts, stowing them in the pocket of her jacket. She would just grab her keys and leave her mother a simple note explaining that she'd changed her mind and decided to drive back to Knoxville, and that she would call tomorrow. Easy as that.

But when she entered the kitchen, she smelled cigarette smoke and heard Carole coughing, and for a second or two Stephanie just stood there, half in the door and half out of it, confused. Then Carole coughed again, muttered, "Damn...," and that helped

Stephanie snap out of her second-long fugue state. She found Carole sitting at the table in the breakfast nook, her legs primly crossed, smoking one of Stephanie's cigarettes and having a difficult time of it.

"Mom... what are you doing?"

"What does it look like I'm doing?" Carole asked, and inexpertly flicked ashes onto a saucer set before her. She took another drag on the cigarette, coughed.

"Since when do you smoke?" Stephanie asked.

Carole glanced at the clock. "Since about five minutes ago."

"And in the house," her daughter pointed out. "You never let *me* smoke inside."

A shrug. "It's my house," Carole said, simply. She held the cigarette up. "How do you smoke these things, Stephanie? They're awful."

"Well, they're menthol." Whether that explained their awfulness or Carole's difficulty smoking them, Stephanie wasn't sure.

Carole nodded, as if it made perfect sense. "I didn't think you'd mind if I took one."

"I don't, but... you don't smoke."

"Maybe I'll start," Carole said, and to punctuate the remark, took another deep drag that ended in a coughing fit.

Stephanie chuckled. "Maybe don't inhale so deep until you get used to it."

Carole tried again, made it without coughing. "How long did it take you to get used to it?"

That made Stephanie laugh. "I was a stupid teenager when I started smoking, Mom," she said. "I thought I was a veteran by my second one."

Carole flicked the ash and it scattered across the table.

Stephanie wiped them into a neat pile, swept them off the table into her palm, then onto the saucer. "Mom, what are you doing? You don't smoke. You think it's disgusting and it stinks, and I'm sure I don't need to remind you—"

"That it causes cancer?" Carole chuckled. "That's funny, isn't it?"

Stephanie was lost. "I don't understand." There. She'd said it.

"I don't either," Carole said, and they stared at one another across the kitchen until Stephanie got tired of standing and slid into the chair facing her mother.

"I mean I *really* don't understand," she said. "Any of this." And she waved a hand in the air between them to mean Carole's sudden interest in smoking.

"And I mean I don't understand *anything*," Carole said, and leaned forward with the force of the confession. "I don't understand how your father could never smoke a day in his life, never drink to excess ever in his life, but he can still die before he even reached middle age." She shrugged. "I don't understand how I, myself, could never smoke or drink and still get cancer. I don't understand how you could start smoking at...what? Fifteen? Sixteen?"

"Sixteen," Stephanie said, and for the first time in her life she realized it as something she should be ashamed of.

"I don't understand how you *can* smoke and drink and here you are now, almost as old as your father was when he got sick, and you're healthy as a horse." Carole shrugged again. "I don't understand how it's determined who lives and who dies. It makes no fucking sense."

Stephanie actually flinched to hear her mother curse, as if she had been slapped.

Carole laughed, not at Stephanie's reaction, but at whatever force at work in the universe that selected who got to stay healthy and who got sick, who lived and who died. "I mean, fourteen kids got *murdered* today. They never got to smoke or drink their lives away, or choose to live healthy, or just do nothing at all. They're dead before they even got to live, and I don't understand it." Another shrug. "I don't understand how someone else got to make that decision for them, and I certainly don't understand how nothing could have happened to the man who killed them all *before* he got to this point today. I mean... why didn't someone shoot him? Why didn't *he* die, like your father? Why didn't *he* get cancer?" Another shrug. "Hell, why was he even born?"

"I don't think it's for us to understand stuff like this," Stephanie said, interjecting herself into her mother's tirade as gently as she could. Her mind was spinning, though. She had never seen her mother like this.

Carole scoffed. "Oh, please, Stephanie." And she laughed. "Are you going to start preaching about God and how He works in mysterious ways, and it's not for us to fathom His intentions? Please..."

"No," Stephanie said. But what had she meant? "It's just... Maybe it's meant to help those of us left behind to grow and become better. You know, as individuals, but also... you know, the whole human race."

Carole laughed again. "You really believe that?" She fixed Stephanie with a hard stare. "You think the human race is getting better by watching itself get sick and die and suffer without any pattern or reason behind it all? I never took you for such a deep thinker."

That stung. "Well, you don't have to insult me," Stephanie said, and heard how weak it sounded as it left her mouth. "I don't understand any of that any more than you do, but I like to think that humanity would move forward from sickness and death and suffering, even without understanding it all, to a place where we would be able to prevent at least some of it from happening." Saying it, she realized that this is what made her breakdown as she heard "The Sweet By-and-By" coming from the church doors during the vigil: not the tragedy of life, but the hope. God, she was a hypocrite, always presenting herself so hard and above it all on the

61

outside, but in reality she was just as scared and hopeful as Tonya Tinker and the woman in the **#PrayForKingston** sweatshirt.

Carole looked down and realized her cigarette had burned out. She gave a small grunt.

"Do you want another one?" Stephanie asked her.

"No, I don't think so." Carole stood. "I think I'll just go to bed."

Stephanie stood, too. "Do you want me to stay?"

And this time Carole shook her head. "No. I want to be alone right now."

"Okay," Stephanie said. Then: "Are you okay, Mom?" She felt the need to ask it, even though she knew the answer.

Carole stopped on her way to the stairs, turned. "No," she said. "I'm not okay. I'm old and I'm tired and I'm pissed off." She nodded toward the light over the table in the breakfast nook. "Make sure you turn all the lights off and lock the door when you go." Then she started for the stairs again.

"I will," Stephanie said. "And I'll call you tomorrow."

Carole didn't respond to that, just shuffled through the den to the stairs and disappeared into the shadows there. Stephanie stood, bewildered, for a long time, her mind a blank. She cleared away the saucer with the cigarette ashes, and the sandwich she had left on the counter. She checked that the front door was locked, and turned the kitchen lights off, made sure the back door would lock behind her, and left her mother's house.

It was just starting to rain as she slid into the driver's seat of her own car, which was a mess compared to Carole's and reeked of stale cigarette smoke, and as she coasted slowly down the driveway she caught herself humming the chorus to "The Sweet By-and-By."

Had

I ran into Tovah at the supermarket, rounding the corner from that no man's land in the center of the store where you can find anything from chocolate bars that weighed a pound to tiki torches to Spanish prayer candles. I needed matches and those were there, too. It was summer and there were grills, lawn chairs, patio umbrellas with hideous floral prints.

Our carts collided. I was looking down at my cell phone. A guy wanted to meet me for drinks and I wasn't so sure.

Tovah cried out. "Oh!"

"Oh my God, I'm so sorry," I said and shoved my phone into my pocket. Then I saw who it was and felt immense relief. She wouldn't make a scene. "Oh, hi, Tovah. Sorry about that. I wasn't looking where I was going."

Tovah just smiled. "Scott's home!" It came out like the chirp of some bird: two quick, staccato notes. I almost didn't understand it, her bird language. She saw the look on my face, and was puzzled why I wasn't smiling like she was. She explained: "He called me yesterday and he flew in this morning, and he'll be here a whole week!" She paused. "Or longer, he said. Maybe."

I nodded, then I asked, "How is he?" I felt I needed to be polite. Scott and I have not spoken, not even by phone, in five years. Maybe six.

Tovah's smile faded. "He didn't call you?"

I shook my head.

"He said he would." She seemed genuinely upset about it. "I asked him, 'Scotty, does Mark know?' and he said he was going to call you. Does he have your number?"

"I think so," I said. My number had not changed. "Maybe not. Maybe he lost it. Maybe he got a new phone and lost it." I wondered who I was trying to convince: Tovah or myself?

She nodded and her orange curls bounced. "Maybe that's it. Do you have his number?"

I caught myself before I said of course I had his number. "I think so." But actually, I know so. It's stored in my phone and I have it written in one of those old address books that no one else in the world has used since the advent of cell phone technology. I have several pages devoted to just Scott, all his old numbers and all his old addresses, going back to high school.

"Okay, *good!*" Tovah was visibly relieved and her smile returned. "He's doing fine, you know. Handsome as ever!" She said this with obvious pride but tried to sound like she was discussing the weather and her lack of control over it. It was sunny; Scott was handsome. She shrugged. What could she do?

I nodded. "I'll give him a call, then." I backed my shopping cart away from Tovah's and noticed for the first time that it was piled with food she would never eat. There were pounds and pounds of red meat: steaks, brisket, ground beef. Scott couldn't eat it all if he stayed a month.

Tovah noticed me looking and grinned sheepishly. "You know how he eats," she said.

"Yeah," I said.

Scott and I met in the back seat of a sixteen-passenger van en route to Myrtle Beach, South Carolina our sophomore year in high school. We were the only two boys on the trip. I had chosen the seat in the back because I didn't really know anyone else in the youth group and thought it might afford me some small measure of solitude on the trip while all the girls whispered and gossiped and cackled like hens toward the front.

Then, through the din of teenage girls, I heard a deep voice declare, "I'm in the back," and there was Scott Miller, his rusty curls reflecting the early morning sunlight as he peered into the depths of the van, saw me sitting in the back, and scowled. He climbed in and squeezed past protesting girls to join me in the back. For some reason, I felt I needed to move to give him more room, but there was nowhere to go. I just made myself smaller there in that back corner.

He looked at me and said, "You're in my chemistry class."

I nodded. "Mrs. Kaplan. Third period."

"Yeah."

He seemed huge to me then. I had grown little since middle school and wouldn't grow much more at all. Scott was already six feet tall and wide at the shoulders, athletic and active and strong. Girls turned into gibbering idiots around him, and I guessed I could understand why, though it was strange for a redhead. There were certainly cuter boys, but there was something about Scott. Or maybe it was just me. Maybe girls acted that way about every guy who played football and basketball and baseball.

"What's your name?" he asked me.

"Mark," I said. "Hoffman," I added, in case it mattered.

He nodded and leaned back as far as he could in the seat, which was maybe two inches. "This is gonna suck," he said, frowning.

"There's probably more room up front," I said, though I hoped he wouldn't go there.

He shook his head. "Nah." Then he kicked his Sebagos off and turned sideways in the seat, his feet pressed against my thigh. I burned hot at the feel of his toes through my shorts. He produced a pair of Wayfarers from somewhere and slid them over his eyes. He did not ask if I was comfortable. I don't think it would have mattered if I told him I wasn't.

He slept all the way to South Carolina, then for some reason the girls decided they would wake him. Their leader, a bossy girl named Mary Jo, with a ponytail and braces, leaned over the seat and screamed, "Oh my God! Scott's asleep! Scott's asleep!" The other girls started a chorus behind her. I failed to see the point.

Scott raised his hand and silenced them. "You're all dumb," he said.

Mary Jo huffed. "*You're* dumb! Who sleeps on a beach trip?"

Behind his sunglasses, Scott rolled his eyes. "We're not at the beach yet."

Mary Jo had no comeback, so she just turned back around, her ponytail whipping the air behind her. I agreed with Scott, though. She was stupid, her and her friends. Supposedly, they were some of the best students at the school, and I guess if you were an academic prodigy, no one really expected you to have much common sense.

"You have a girlfriend?"

It was Scott. He was talking to me. "Me?"

He grinned. His teeth were perfect, straight and white. He could do toothpaste commercials and run the tip of his tongue over those teeth and declare how great it felt and everyone would believe him and want to die because their teeth were nothing like his. Mine were nothing like his. "Yeah, you."

I shook my head and pushed my glasses up on the bridge of my nose.

"Good for you," he said, and I wasn't sure what he meant by that, because it might be sarcasm.

"Do you?" I asked, and tried to sound like I had gone on the defensive, like how dare he question my virility, my ability to find a girlfriend, my sexuality. My voice cracked, though, so I doubt he felt challenged.

He shrugged. "I have a few." And that was it. He was silent the rest of the way. Mary Jo left him alone, and I read my book in the corner.

When we arrived at the house in Myrtle Beach, I was both thrilled and terrified knowing I would be sharing a room with him for five days. He took the bed closest to the doors that opened onto the patio, but I did not argue because I would, at some point, see him in his underwear.

There was no real agenda that week in Myrtle Beach. The trip was our reward for raising more money than we needed, and our sponsors treated us with a week at the beach: no meetings, no seminars, no schedule really at all, except that we had to return to the house for lunch and dinner.

I was at a loss immediately, never having had so much free time to myself. The girls were out the door first thing in the morning, intent on cultivating suntans that would carry them through the remainder of the school year and make other girls envious. Scott slept late, sprawled across his bed in a tangle of sheets. I used to the time to steal glimpses of him in his underwear, pretending to be asleep myself on my side of the room. He did not wear cheap Fruit of the Loom or Hanes, no. Scott's were Jockey. Expensive and athletic.

69

When he finally left the bed, it was to pee in the private bathroom off our room. He left the door open. I was scandalized and delighted at the same time.

"Let's go to the beach, Mark," he said when he was finished.

"Um. Okay..." I did not linger over my surprise at having him include me in his plans. I jumped up, fished my trunks out of my suitcase, and escaped to the bathroom.

We went to the beach and lay on hideously colored towels in sight of the house. Scott stripped away his shirt and plopped down; I was more conscious of my body and all its shortcomings. I left my t-shirt on.

"You working on a farmer's tan?" Scott asked me, his lips pressed against his towel.

"Oh. No." I peeled off my own shirt and waited to be mocked. Scott either didn't notice or didn't care, because he said nothing. I relaxed a bit, but I was certain everyone on the beach had an opinion about my skinny arms, my ribs, my paleness. I had brought my book and decided to hide behind it.

Scott, though fair skinned and red haired, spent more time with his shirt off than I did and was the color of honey under all his freckles. I cut glances at him over my book, the muscles in his back moving with the rise and fall of his breathing, the way the hair on his legs shone like gold, his fingers digging into the sand to each side of his Spuds McKenzie beach towel. I wanted him to ask me to rub lotion on his back.

"You read too much," he said, his eyes closed.

"I have a report," I explained.

He chuckled. "Yeah, I do, too. That's what Cliff's Notes are for."

Overhead, gulls swooped and cried. Down the beach, closer to the water, children shrieked with glee at the discovery of a jellyfish. "Teachers read the Cliff's Notes, too, you know," I told him. I was not going to let him be better than me at everything.

He opened one eye and scowled at me. "Yeah, so you paraphrase. Duh."

I shook my head. "That's cheating. Kind of. I'd rather read the book and explain it in my own words." God, I sounded like a dweeb.

Scott just laughed. "Whatever."

These were our conversations, mainly. Only the subject matter changed. He derided my choice in music, in movies, in clothes ("You dress like a dork, man.") I endured it just to be close to him and call myself his friend, though I suspected he hardly felt the same about me. I wasn't stupid. But after years of being taunted by guys just like him, I was sharing a room with him in Myrtle Beach. I had seen him in his underwear. I was watching him sunbathe, memorizing every inch of him. How could we not be best buds after this week? I was convinced we would return home and be inseparable.

That night, though, after dinner and what passed for "lights out" with our permissive chaperones, Scott told me he was going out. "Where?" I asked. "It's, like, midnight."

He shrugged. "Walking on the beach."

"Oh." I waited for him to tell me to put my book down and come with him, like earlier when he'd told me we were going to the beach. That's what best buds did.

Instead, he put on a clean shirt and combed his hair in the bathroom mirror.

"What if someone asks where you went?" I asked.

He gave me a look in the mirror. "What, you're gonna rat me out?"

"No, but what if?"

He left the bathroom and gave my head a shove as he passed me on his way out. "They won't ask." He seemed sure of it. I did, too. People like Scott were lucky that way. They did things and never got caught. He flashed me a smile just before he slipped out through the French doors. "Don't wait up." Then he was gone. I listened to his footsteps across the deck and down the stairs that led to the beach and realized I was furious at him. Why didn't he ask me to come? Didn't he want to hang out? We were supposed to be friends.

I sat up late, well into the morning, reading. When I finally decided he wasn't coming back any time soon, it was almost three o'clock and I could barely keep my eyes open. I turned off the light and was almost asleep when it occurred to me to check the French doors to make sure they weren't locked so he could get back in. Then I went to bed, my mind made up to hate him when I saw him next.

Scott would either call or he wouldn't. He'd always been that way: he was your friend, or maybe not. When he was with you, it was clear; when he wasn't, you could never be sure.

The rest of the Myrtle Beach trip was much of the same. The girls disappeared in the morning to bake themselves in the sun. Scott and I stayed closer to the beach house and barely spoke. I was mad, but he was oblivious or couldn't care less. "Let's take a walk," he'd say, and we went for a walk. I figured he was checking out girls, and I always expected them to come running up to him to plan their midnight rendezvous in whispered tones while I stood nearby, skinny and irrelevant. I understood perfectly all the stares he got as we strolled along the beach, just at the water's edge: he was both textbook all-American male and an anomaly—a red haired object of desire. Like if Opie Taylor had grown up and turned into James Dean.

I saw men checking him out, too. They tended to be older, effeminate, their bushy mustaches in stark contrast to the voices that issued from the lips they covered. "Does the carpet match the drapes, honey?" I heard as we walked. Scott kept walking, but I had to turn and see who dared be so brazen in public like that. Of course, it was a group of men gathered under two enormous rainbow beach umbrellas or sunning themselves and I could not identify the speaker. I wondered myself if the carpets matched the drapes, and burned with both the desire to know and the shame of realizing that I wanted to.

One night we walked along The Strip and it was the beach all over again, only this time we were wearing more clothes, and I was more of a nuisance to Scott. I could tell. "I don't feel like it," he said when I suggested we check out the arcade at The Gay Dolphin gift shop. Something about the name of the place made me mildly angry.

Then I suggested we check out some of the t-shirt shops. "They do airbrushing," I pointed out. All of them did, though, so it really was no big deal. And I didn't actually want an airbrushed t-shirt—I thought they were particularly tacky, always a sunset and palm trees in silhouette with your name (and, if you were lucky, the name of your significant other) in a ridiculous cursive script at a forty-five degree angle.

Scott wasn't interested. "You go ahead."

I scowled at him. "Well, what are you going to do?"

He shrugged. "Probably just walk around."

I was instantly as angry as I had been the night he sneaked out and didn't come back until three in the morning. I suspected drugs or alcohol, probably both. Probably sex, too. I decided not to care; if he could do it, so could I. I just shrugged and said, "Whatever." And I left him standing there on the sidewalk and went in search of some kitschy gift from The Gay Dolphin to take home to my mother.

The place was like someone had the bright idea to take everything from an outdoor flea market and drag it inside, cram it onto creaky shelves, then spray paint it "beach colors" (turquoise, yellow, orange) and sprinkle it with glitter. I knew my mother would feign pleasure with anything I brought her, and I could have grabbed the first thing I saw—a cheap, plaster of Paris lighthouse that looked like a preschool art project—but I turned it into a chore, because it gave me time to keep watching the door and the sidewalk outside to see if Scott was going to reconsider and follow me inside.

He didn't, of course. I walked back outside and scanned the sidewalk for that familiar mop of rusty curls, but he was nowhere in sight. A mild panic gripped me. Not for his safety, I knew he'd be fine, sneaking in around three o'clock. I was worried that I'd pissed him off, that he wouldn't understand that I actually did care, and that he wouldn't want to hang out with me anymore during our remaining time in Myrtle Beach. Stupid shit, and I knew it, but I went in search of him anyway, from one side of The Strip to the other, up and down both sides of the street.

I tried to think where he would go. Where were alcohol and drugs for teenagers found at the beach? I considered the hotels as I jogged past them, my boat shoes slapping against the sidewalk and the soles of my feet stinging inside them. Hotels would mean parents or chaperones, supervision; noise would alert others, and there was the risk of police.

75

In the movies, kids went to the beach to do things they weren't supposed to do, usually around a campfire or behind a rocky outcrop. There was always beer, sometimes liquor, and more often than not there was a bag of weed and sex. I wasn't worried that I would forever be labeled The Square if I crashed some beach bonfire where Scott was frolicking with big-breasted girls and a couple of six packs. I hurried there, got sand in my shoes, and gave up immediately. There were no bonfires, just darkness stretching in both directions. I went back to The Pavilion and half-heartedly played Galaga and Centipede until the place started to empty out, then I sulked back to the beach house and went in through the French doors into our room.

Scott was there in the morning. I never heard him come in, but there he was, sleeping soundlessly. I glared at his exposed back, adorned with fading scratch marks at his sides and shoulders. It didn't take a genius to know what had caused them, but I was infuriated as I dressed and left the house. I had no particular destination in mind, so I ended up on the beach. I took my shoes off and started walking toward downtown Myrtle Beach, intent on keeping my mind off Scott. I saw the seagulls and dead or dying jellyfish the size of babies washed up on the beach. I said hi to an old couple walking by in sweat suits, even though it was already close to ninety degrees and it made no sense.

I walked until the bottoms of my feet felt raw from the sand, and was just about to turn around when I saw a guy in a Speedo coming toward me with a dog on a leash. He smiled at me as he passed, and I smiled back, and then I heard "Hey, where's your friend?"

I turned. "Huh?"

He laughed. "I asked where your friend was," he said, and closed the distance between us. His dog, an indecipherable breed, sniffed at my bare feet, my shoes in my hand. "The redhead."

"Oh." I felt myself scowl. Then I shrugged. I just couldn't think of a convincing lie that quickly.

"Yeah, we saw you guys walk by the other day." Up close, he was really thin, his chest almost sunken. A thin, gold hoop glinted in one nipple and I felt something like yearning rise into my throat. "I'm Greg." And he held out a hand.

I shook it, I hoped firmly. "Mark." I had never been so close to an actual gay man before, and I'm not counting the guy, Rick, who cut my mom's hair back home. My mind was spinning even though my vision had never been clearer. I saw tiny lines feathering out from the corners of his eyes, which were brown; I saw a thin gold chain around his neck; I saw that ring in his nipple again and I heard myself ask "That hurt?"

He laughed and glanced down at it, gave it a flick. "Not really." Then, "Well, a little at first, I guess. But now it's nothing."

"Cool," I said, because that was what you were supposed to say when there was nothing else to say.

"Yeah," Greg said and smiled, and his teeth were big. "Hey, so we're having a party tonight, you should come." He pointed past me and I turned to look. "That house there, the one with the pirate flag."

Sure enough, there was an actual Jolly Roger flying from the roof of a modern-looking beach house with tall windows and redwood shingles. "Cool," I said again.

Greg chuckled. "Yeah. Just a bunch of us guys having fun, you know?" He was looking at me pretty hard, like he expected a certain response and was waiting for me to give it. I was in awe that he either had no idea I was fifteen-years-old, or he knew and just didn't care.

"What time?"

Greg shrugged his skinny shoulders. "Whenever, really. There's no set time." He gave the dog's leash a jerk and started to turn away, then glanced back and said, "Oh, and bring your friend."

I should have known that was coming. I just gnashed my teeth and turned it into a smile. "Yeah. I'll tell him."

"Cool," Greg said, and it sounded exactly the way I had said it earlier. Then he was walking away, the dog lumbering along behind him, and I saw that he had some kind of tattoo on his right shoulder.

Three years later, when we are both freshmen in college—Scott at Tulane and me at Emory—and home for the winter break, Scott will come out to me across a plate of fried calamari at what, at the time, was the hottest Italian restaurant in town. I was struck dumb by the announcement. He laughed. "I thought you knew," he said.

78

"How was I supposed to know?"

And he reminded me about that trip to Myrtle Beach, all those nights he'd snuck out and crept back in of a morning—what had I thought he'd been out doing? And had I not thought it odd that he never asked me to come along? I did not dare tell him that it had infuriated me. "I was meeting other boys who were sneaking out," he said, like he was telling me he'd gone to see the sunrise or pick flowers.

"Oh," was all I could manage. I'd assumed he was sneaking out to meet girls.

"And that one party," he added after a pause for thought, through a mouthful of squid. "It was a group of older guys. They were staying in one of the houses up the beach from us."

I instantly recalled Greg and his Speedo and his nipple ring, and I felt my face flush. Greg had invited me to that same party but I had chickened out at the last minute, standing in the dark at the bottom of the wooden steps that climbed from the beach to the house. I stood there and heard raucous laughter, shouts, music (Madonna, if I remember correctly) and thought I might actually vomit, my anxiety was so bad. Various scenes played through my head, and none of them ended well for me: I would be given some drink laced with something and be rendered unconscious and awaken hours later, naked and sore, having been taken advantage of by any number of strange men; or the police would come and there I would be, drunk or high or both, and have to explain to my parents via phone from the Myrtle Beach police station why I had been arrested and where I had been; or, the least reprehensible but still shameful—I would be exposed as underage and be ordered away from the party.

Oh, I had wanted to go, to be there amongst Greg and all his friends, who were older and better looking and more desirable than I, at fifteen, was. I had imagined them all tattooed, with nipple rings, walking around in Speedos even though there was no sun, sipping drinks with names that suggested sex—and me in their center, reveling in the forbiddenness of it all—but as I put my foot on that bottom step to start the climb up, I saw that Jolly Roger and all the yearning just went out of me like the air out of a balloon. Instead I just sat down and examined my misery.

Then I was still thinking Scott was out fucking girls and I wanted to be that bold and unwavering, only with boys. To be told later that he was at that very party, had no doubt experienced it the very way that I had hoped to experience it, had the effect of a mild stroke: it rendered my mind so blank, that I actually came to my senses several minutes later and wasn't sure how I came to be sitting across from Scott, sharing a plate of calamari.

"What?" he'd asked me. There must have been some look on my face.

"Nothing," I said, and almost laughed because it was so true. There was literally nothing in my head at that moment.

He shrugged. "Okay. So, I was thinking we'd hit the bars after dinner. Burkhart's, Crazy Ray's..."

"Sure," I said, because I had nothing else to say in the wake of learning that Scott was gay.

We went to Crazy Ray's first, armed with our fake IDs, because it was still early and it tended to be quieter and no one would be working the door. Scott metamorphosed the second we were through the door. On the sidewalk he was still the hyper-masculine jock from high school, strutting around like the world was a locker room, then he turned into a flaming queen the second the door shut behind us. "Girl, I need a cocktail!" he declared, and sashayed to the bar where he leaned in on both elbows with his ass sticking out. I was struck by a curious mixture of shock and shame. I tried to remember if I'd ever been called "girl" in my life.

"Vodka and cranberry," he was telling the bartender.

"Cape Cod," the bartender said as he smiled and gave Scott a long once over. "Coming right up."

"And one of those, too!" Scott said and waved his arms like he was trying to be seen in the last row of the upper balcony. The bartender—Frank, I think—laughed like he had never heard anything so funny in his life.

"Can I get a Heineken?" I called to his back.

"Sure thing," he called back, without so much as a glance in my direction.

From the look on Scott's face, you would have thought I'd asked for the blood of a newborn. "Beer?"

He spat the word, like it might make him sick if it stayed in his mouth.

"Yeah," I said, with a laugh. "So what?"

"It's just so... redneck." Again with the flailing of the arms.

I rolled my eyes just as dramatically. "It's a beer, Scott."

"It's so *unsophisticated.*"

Frank set the Cape Cod down in front of Scott, then reached below the bar for my beer. "Oh, I see. You drink like a sixty-year-old queen on Fire Island now, and that makes you a socialite? Can I still call you 'Scott,' or do I have to call you 'Zsa Zsa?'" Frank heard it and laughed.

Scott was clearly miffed. "Whatever," he said, like every bitchy girl we had ever gone to high school with, and grabbed his drink and took a sip through the straw. I could not believe what I was seeing, but this was what Scott had become since going away to Tulane. No one knew him there, so he got to become someone—*something*—else: a flamboyantly gay example of life in the closet. Sure, he had come out to me, but I knew the minute we left the bar, he would turn back into that macho, swaggering jock I had come to know.

I drank my beer and we stood in silence, until a couple of guys walked up to the bar. One of them made no attempt whatsoever to hide the fact that he liked what he saw when he looked at Scott, who turned to me and whispered, "What do you think of that one?"

I looked around him to the guy. He was older, maybe mid-to-late thirties, mustached, and clearly spent as much time as possible working out. His bicep straining against the pique of his polo shirt made me think of David Banner transforming into The Incredible Hulk and ripping his clothing to shreds in the process.

"God, don't make it so obvious!" Scott hissed around his straw.

"He's not my type," I said.

Scott just shrugged. "He can be had."

This was his way of saying he wanted to fuck the guy in question and it would be easy for him to make that happen. As if he even needed to tell me that. All he really needed to do was walk up to the guy and tell him he wanted to have sex, and I'm pretty sure it would be a done deal. Both guys were checking him out, and me too, I suppose, but only wondering what such a glorious specimen of young all-American manhood was doing with such a nerd. I drank my beer and pretended to be oblivious.

At Burkhart's later that night, it was worse. There were more men and Scott had more alcohol in his system. "That one can be had," he said, over and over.

"Then go talk to him," I said, my exasperation unmistakable.

83

He responded as if I'd suggested he throw himself into a volcano. "No!" he said. "I want *them* to come to *me*. I don't want to look desperate."

I actually laughed. I guess remarking that practically every guy who walked by could be had wasn't desperate at all. "Sounds like a solid plan," I told him, and went for another beer. Of course the bartender asked who my friend was. I felt like cracking his skull with my empty beer bottle. "Just a friend from high school."

"He's cute."

I made a noise that could only be described as the love child of a laugh and a snort of derision. "Yeah, he knows it, too." I took my beer and didn't leave him a tip.

In the meanwhile, Scott had disappeared. I figured he'd gone to the bathroom after slugging all those Cape Cods, so I stood where we'd been standing and waited for him. No one checked me out the way they had checked Scott out, and I kept telling myself I was fine with that. But I wasn't really. It would be nice to be wanted like that, but I had not really grown into anything more than a freshman in college at that point, which basically meant I still looked and acted much the same as I had in high school. I was short, I'd put on weight in college eating junk food in the dorm all the time, and I still dressed like my mother bought all my clothes. "Bookish nerd" was not an accepted gay type. I might as well have been invisible.

When Scott didn't come back, I got concerned for about a second, then I got pissed. I made up my mind then and there that I was not going to spend my entire night chasing him around a gay bar while he went on his manhunt. I would find him and tell him I was ready to go; he could come with me, or he could get a cab.

I found him at the back bar, surrounded by more of his kind: lean, athletic, good-looking men with the right hair and clothes who were what Scott would become in a few years. They were doing shots of tequila. "Mark!" Scott called in that same voice he'd used when he'd called me "girl" earlier. The men around him shouted my name, too. It sounded like a battle cry. "We're doing shots!"

"Yeah, I see," I said. No one offered me one.

Scott leaned in and whispered "And I am about ten seconds away from being wasted." His breath smelled like a frat party I'd attended my first week at Emory.

"Yeah, I see that, too." I decided not to mince my words. "Look, if you're good here, I'm gonna head out. I have an essay due." That last part was a lie, but I didn't care.

For a brief, brief second Scott looked panicked. I had driven us, so if I left now he would either have to go with me or he was at the mercy of taxis and mass transit, neither of which he was comfortable with. People like Scott did not take cabs and buses and trains; someone might see. "Well, okay...," he said, but he was far from okay.

One of the guys threw an arm around his shoulder. "Don't worry, honey. You're safe with us."

He turned to me. "We'll take real good care of him, sweetie. You go on home."

I hated being called "sweetie" and I hated the slightly insulting tone with which he told me to go on home—like I was the only underage person there. But whatever. Scott said, "I'll call you tomorrow, Mark." Then he took another shot and I doubted he would be doing much of anything tomorrow but explaining to his mom and dad where he had been all night and why he smelled like a bar rag.

"Whatever," I said, and turned and left. I was no idiot; I knew very well he would end up in one of their beds and lie to his parents about where he was. He would tell them he had stayed the night at my dorm room, and they would believe him. Nothing ever changed with Scott. Well, except the fact that he was gay now. That was a new one.

Scott still hadn't called, but I kept reminding myself that he'd always been like that: he would say he'd call, and he might or he might not; if he did, it was usually at the last minute. And it was typical of me to sit around waiting for him to call, too, so if I was going to be pissed at him I would have to be pissed at myself. He'd probably just told Tovah that to get her off his back anyway. "Are you going to call Mark, Scotty?" I could hear her ask him, and his response, exasperated: "Yeah yeah yeah. I'll call him." Chances were he had never intended to call.

The last time we'd seen each other had been terse, at best. Well, it had been his father's funeral, so that was part of it, but two years before that I had, in a drunken stupor, declared my undying love for him in the parking lot of Burkhart's.

He had laughed.

"What's so funny?" I had asked, grinning myself.

"You," he'd said, supporting me as he aimed his car's remote into the air and clicked it repeatedly in search of his car.

"Well, I do," I said, and took advantage of the closeness of our bodies to nuzzle his shoulder with my forehead. "Always have."

He just laughed again. "You're drunk," he said. *Click click, click click.* In the distance, his car horn responded with a short bark. "Aha!" He steered me in that direction.

"Yeah, but I know what I'm saying," I said, and nuzzled some more. I could smell his deodorant, and beneath it a scent that was only him, something like the smell of leaves in the fall. "I love you. I have for as long as I've known you." And for good measure, I added those years up in my addled brain. "Ten years. That's a long time"

"You're just drunk, Mark," he said. "You're not in love with me."

I pulled away from him. "Don't tell me what I feel," I said. In my mind I snapped it, but it came out a slur, like someone had slowed down the speed on the recording of me snapping at him. "I've been in love with you since that trip to Myrtle Beach, I just kept it to myself because I thought you were straight." Here I raised a finger. "But, as fate would have it, you're *not* straight! You're as queer as I am. Queer as a three dollar bill." Something my mom said to describe the guy who cut her hair.

He reached for me. "C'mon, Mark."

I dodged his hand. "No, let's talk about this. I need to get this out," I said. Really, what I needed—what I *wanted*—was to say all this and have him realize that yes, he loved me too, and always had. Then we would fall into each other's arms there in that parking lot as cars moved around us on all sides and kiss, and it wouldn't be as romantic as standing on a beach with the sun setting or rising behind us, or on the street in the middle of Times Square, or on a bridge over the Seine, but hey—you took it where you could get it. "I'm in love with you, Scott. There. Now what do you have to say to that?"

"I say you're drunk," he said, and grabbed me hard by one arm and dragged me toward his car. "I say you're drunk and you're making a fool out of yourself *and* me, now get in the car." He led me around to the passenger's side, tore open the door, and shoved me in.

I heard laughter from outside the car, and someone asked, "He gonna be okay?"

And Scott answered, "Nothing a good night's sleep won't fix."

"Bless his heart," the other voice said, and it made me furious.

Scott got into the driver's seat and started the engine. The radio blared. He made a sound of disgust and turned it off. The silence was nearly as deafening.

"So you're embarrassed by me?" I asked.

"Yes," he said, quick and to the point. "You're drunk and you don't know what you're saying. You'd never say shit like that if you were sober."

Well, that much was true. "I know what I'm saying," I said, and my voice sounded small. Like we were in an auditorium and not the confines of a Honda. "Just because I'm drunk doesn't mean I don't mean what I'm saying."

Scott grunted. "But you shouldn't be saying it at all," he said, and clutched the steering wheel with both his hands. I watched his pink knuckles turn white as bone.

"No, I *should* be saying it," I countered. "And you need to hear it."

"No, I don't."

I just nodded.

"Because you don't mean it," he went on. "It's not you saying it, it's those ten beers you drank. You *think* you're in love with me. That's what alcohol does. It... it distorts things. You just *think* you're in love with me."

This was going nowhere. Even through the fog of the alcohol, I could see that. "No. The beer's just giving me the courage to say what I've wanted to say for years."

"Well, you should have kept it to yourself."

"Why?" I stared hard at him. His face went in and out of focus: his mouth in a tight frown, his forehead wrinkled.

He laughed, but there was no mirth in it. "Because," he said.

It was my turn to make a sound of disgust. "That's weak," I told him.

"Because I don't feel the same way," he said. "We're friends. Or... I *thought* we were, and now you go lay this shit on me." He slapped the steering wheel. "And it wouldn't be so bad if you weren't drunk, but you're drunk and you can't even take no for an answer. You just keep pushing. I'm trying to be nice here, Mark."

In that instant, the pounding of the blood in my head stopped. I couldn't even hear the car's engine as we idled there in the long queue of cars waiting to exit onto Piedmont. "Then don't be nice," I said. "Say what you want to say." A voice in my head screamed at me that I would regret that, but it was too late. There was no taking it back.

Scott sighed. "Just forget it."

"No," I said. "You started it, now finish it. Say what you want to say." I waited a second, then added: "I'm drunk, remember. I won't remember any of this in the morning."

He threw me a look, then his features softened and he tried to smile, but it just didn't work the way he wanted it to. He sighed again and said, "You're not my type." He might as well have punched me in the face. "You're not my type, Mark, and you know it."

I waited for him to go on, but when it became clear that he had said all that he felt he needed to say, I laughed. It even hurt my ears, it was so loud and harsh. "Your *type?*" I asked, and laughed some more. "You actually have a *type*, Scott? I thought you just fucked anything that moved. Right? 'He can be had,' right? That's the criteria, isn't it?" I watched the muscles in his jaw work as he clenched his teeth, and the muscles in his forearm contract as he gripped the steering wheel. I could only assume he did it to keep from punching me. "That's a good one, Scott." I laughed some more. Scott said nothing. What could he say? He'd said it all, and he was right. I wasn't his type. And I was right, too: Scott would have sex with any man he could seduce, except for me.

It occurred to me then to get out of the car, but it was easier said than done. I fought with the seatbelt, then I couldn't find the door handle, then when I was actually out of the car, I realized I didn't have any particular destination in mind.

"Where are you going, Mark?" Scott asked, just as I slammed the door.

"Home," I said, which was idiotic. I was nowhere near the Emory campus.

The window slid down. "Get back in the car," Scott told me.

I ignored him and started walking toward a nearby pharmacy. He called after me a few times, but I kept walking and he finally gave up. I saw him drive by as I asked a drag queen in a silver wig and eyelashes if she could help me call a cab. "A cab or an ambulance, honey?" She ended up driving me home and her car smelled like coconut incense. When she dropped me off, she told me to come see her show the following night at Burkhart's. I knew I shouldn't make a promise that I wouldn't keep, but I said I would.

Scott and I did not speak for two years, until his father's funeral, and neither of us mentioned the scene in the parking lot of Burkhart's. He spoke first. "Thanks for coming," he said. We were on the patio at the back of his parents' house. It was sunny, but cold.

"I'm sorry." We did not look at each other. I stared at the torn black ribbon pinned to his lapel; Scott stared into the house where Tovah sat with their rabbi, surrounded by the mourners, sharing memories of her husband. I realized then I had no real memories of Scott's father, except that he had never said much. And was I apologizing for what happened the last time we spoke, or just being polite and saying what I was expected to say at a shiva?

He nodded.

Later that night, he called me and asked if I wanted to go out, and desperate for his forgiveness (or something), I immediately said yes. We did not go to Burkhart's, thank God. Instead we went to a smaller, quieter place in East Atlanta that was roughly the size of my new apartment. I expected Scott to be somber and brooding in the wake of his father's passing, but he was the exact opposite. "I need a cocktail in the worst way," he said as he flopped against the bar and started making eyes at the bartender.

I heaved an enormous sigh and climbed onto the stool next to him.

Dating had always filled me with a mild terror, not unlike a trip to the dentist as a child. Too much was unknown and unforeseeable, and I wanted to control the outcome from the beginning. It was an absurd notion, I knew, and therefore avoided dating as much as possible. In my life I had only been in two relationships of any length, and both of those were years apart—the first in my early twenties, the second when I was thirty. Neither lasted longer than two years. In between I dated with little enthusiasm or practiced celibacy with the same minimal fervor. I watched Scott and wanted to be like him, but didn't really know how to go about it. The easy control he had over his own sexuality intrigued and alarmed me, and I could only guess that he had decided the guidelines we were given, as gay males, in those days to protect ourselves and our partners from illness simply did not apply to him.

Scott had more sex in one month than I did the entire time we were in college. I knew this by learning to catch the things he said in passing, never outright. For instance, I would make some remark about being shunned by the gay population of Atlanta because I had refused an invitation to a sex party in my building, and Scott would say, "You should have gone. They're not so bad," so I knew he had been to one, or several.

I tried to get more details—"How would you know they're not so bad?"—but he would just shrug and move on to something else: how he was considering dropping basketball and losing his scholarship, or where he might go in Europe for Spring Break. Later, I might jokingly bring up crabs as I purchased a tube of itch cream and he might make a comment about getting rid of all my bedclothes and underwear and buying new everything. I imagined his sex life to be identical to every gay porn I had ever seen in my life, all the men as taut and tanned and endowed as the ridiculously named porn stars, and Scott at their center—shopping for shoes or working out or simply going to check the mail and ending up in a torrid three-way or orgy, complete with pulsing synthesizer.

My own experiences were as graceless and clumsy as I was, made more so by my crippling fear of infection. My one late-night visit to a bookstore—over a year in the planning and execution—resulted in my relenting to be sucked off by an obese, older man with greasy, thinning hair in his car in the parking lot, and left me feeling so contaminated and paralyzed I could barely function. I went to be tested the next morning and was told by the very patient, smiling nurse that not only would the test reveal nothing after such a short time, but that I had probably not been exposed to anything at all. "You can always come back later," she said.

"How much later?" I asked, because I had to know.

She shrugged and told me a couple of weeks. I marked it in my day planner and was there waiting for them to open. I then spent the next week in agony, convinced that my results would be positive, and planning how I would explain it to my parents. The nurse was right, of course. The results came back negative and I was so relieved, I actually burst into tears and fell into a period of celibacy so stringent I would have been a candidate for sainthood had I been a Christian. It was broken with the advent of internet dating—which is what we called it, although it was really just a front for a level of promiscuity unseen since Caligula.

Again I tried, and again I failed. So I stayed off the personals sites and out of the chat rooms and settled for Scott's reports from the front lines. I listened, appalled and intrigued as he told me of sexual exploits I could only think of: in bathrooms at restaurants and bars, in his car in parking lots, at work. In my head, as I had screamed at him outside Burkhart's so long ago, I imagined he had very low standards, but apparently he drew the line at some things. Smokers, for one.

"So, you'll bareback, but you won't kiss someone who smokes?" I asked him. I needed to understand this.

Scott gave a dramatic roll of his eyes. "When you actually have a sex life, Mark, then you can judge me."

I laughed. "It just doesn't make sense. Are you afraid kissing a smoker will give you lung cancer?"

"Whatever." His final word on anything he could not explain.

Ultimately, I would be glad for those extended periods of self-imposed chastity, but not while I was experiencing them. Guys would talk to me—albeit guys who were nothing whatsoever like the ones talking to Scott—and I would turn into a prude, or a liar, or I would say everything wrong and watch, both disappointed and relieved, as their loss of interest swept across their faces. Apparently I could not, to borrow Scott's phrase of choice, be had.

"Just do it," Scott told me. "There's nothing wrong with having sex with people, Mark. If you're interested and they're interested, then why be so cagey about it?"

"I'd rather be selective," I told him, which was a lie, because I wanted nothing more than to be unrestrained; I just wanted to be a whore without consequences.

When I did give in and sleep with someone I hardly knew, even though I used a condom, I was a nervous wreck in the days and weeks that followed, convinced that even the slightest sniffle or the least pain in my back or neck were the first signs of a fever coming on, heralding seroconversion illness. I caught people staring as I felt for swollen lymph nodes, usually as I sat at work or waited in line at a deli. Testing had evolved and no longer took a week to get the results, but the twenty minutes I waited in my doctor's exam room seemed just as interminable, and each time I vowed never to have sex again. I wondered if Scott had these episodes, then admonished myself. Of course he didn't. Scott was wanton and perfectly fine with that. I was the puritan.

Part of me still believed there was a chance for me and Scott, and I was actually ashamed of myself when I realized it, even as I suggested to him that we take a trip to Provincetown. "You know, like that trip to Myrtle Beach in high school," I said. "Only this time, we're both out so there's no need for sneaking around."

"Provincetown?" he asked me, and even through the phone I could hear the doubt in his voice and picture the look on his face.

"Yeah. It'll be fun!" I directed him to a web site and he still seemed reluctant when he agreed that it looked like fun.

I booked the cottage and my flight to Boston. We would meet at the airport and take the ferry out together for the long Labor Day weekend. I decided if there was ever going to be anything between us, this was my last chance, even as I recalled his words to me that night in the parking lot of Burkhart's when I'd bared my soul to him: *You're not my type.* I dressed better now, and braces had corrected my teeth. I made a good effort to work out and eat properly, but exercise bored me and fast food was just too convenient. I would never be built like Scott—or the men he preferred; I was average height, which meant if I gained five pounds there was nowhere for it to go, so it went directly to my midsection. I dressed to disguise it, and it was amazing what the right clothing could do. Of course, that led me to panic about my weight. We would be at the beach. I would not be able to hide my pudge under hoodies and sweaters.

I resolved to work out and starve myself until I dropped five pounds. I lasted three days.

My flight landed first, so I collected my luggage and waited as close to the baggage claim as I could. I missed Scott when he arrived, but he noticed me immediately. He was wearing a baseball cap and sunglasses, and I told myself that was why I didn't recognize him. He was thin, though, thinner than I had ever seen him. "I didn't recognize you," I blurted out as he swept me into a polite hug. He felt thin, too.

Scott just laughed. "Good thing I recognized you, then."

"I'm fat now," I said. Might as well get it out in the open before he said it and made me feel bad.

"Whatever," he said, like he had always said. "You are *so* not fat."

We caught the ferry out to Provincetown, and I did most of the talking. Scott was on his phone, texting, but he would give me a nod or say "Yeah?" or grunt every now and then. I shared all the research I had done—on the cottage I'd rented for us, on where we might eat, the nightlife. "And I plan to hit Herring Cove beach first thing," I declared, surprised at myself for saying it aloud. I'd talked myself into and out of it for a month, and even as I disembarked the plane in Boston I had convinced myself that I had no business at a nude beach.

"Sounds like fun," Scott said, his tone one of supreme disinterest. He did not glance up from his phone.

We rode the rest of the way in silence. I stared out the ferry at Massachusetts Bay, at Cape Cod as we approached it, at anything but Scott on his fucking phone. On the deck, a group of men laughed and mocked one another, their voices shrill. I envied them and found myself standing and heading in their direction.

"Where you going?" Scott asked, though he really didn't seem all that concerned.

"Outside," I said. "I'll be right back." Unless I could help it, but I didn't add that part. He would be fine with his phone.

I got a beer from the snack bar and found a seat as close to the men as I could without seeming too conspicuous, but really it wouldn't have mattered if I'd planted myself right in their midst. They were oblivious to anything but one another, and I found myself laughing at them as they insulted one another, then fell into a giant group hug, only to start the insults anew as they came out of it. I envied them, their cattiness and their closeness.

Inside, Scott was talking on his phone, nodding and smiling.

We walked from the ferry landing to the cottage on Commercial Street in the West End. I had chosen it and paid for it, Scott telling me "Just pick one! I'll be fine with whatever!" But I knew from the look on his face that he had expected to be closer to Downtown Provincetown and the gay bars.

"This place is awesome, don't you think?" I asked, staring out the French doors to the Atlantic, literally fifty feet from the door. "It was built in the 1930s, but it's totally updated."

Scott gave a shrug as he walked past me to select which room would be his. "It's kind of isolated, don't you think?" I knew he really meant it wasn't close to the gay bars and the nightlife.

I laughed. "There isn't ten feet between this cottage and the ones on either side of it," I said. "That's hardly isolated. It isn't like we're on a deserted island ten miles out to sea." I decided the room with the view of the ocean was going to be mine and deposited my suitcase on the bed.

"Whatever," Scott said, and disappeared into the bedroom on the opposite side of the house.

I was already imagining him refusing to pay his half of the cottage because he didn't like the location and caught myself getting angered at just the thought. Then I thought, *Maybe he won't even stay here, if he's that unhappy with it.* If he met some guy and shacked up at a hotel downtown for the entire weekend, then I would have the entire place to myself and that actually wouldn't be so bad. I unpacked and used the time to calm down.

"I'm going to the beach," I told him when I was finished. "You coming?"

Scott glanced up from his phone. "It's right outside." He flicked his eyes in that direction.

"Herring Cove," I said.

He shook his head. "I'm gonna head into town, get a cocktail."

I shrugged. "See you later, then."

I made it a point to act like it was no big deal, and by the time I reached Herring Cove it actually wasn't. A sign there stated that nudity was a violation of some federal statute, so I would have to be uninhibited some other way. Maybe I would sleep with a different guy every night, which is what I imagined Scott to be working on via his iPhone and some hookup site. Maybe I would find an orgy and make up for that missed opportunity back in Myrtle Beach all those years ago. Of course, I had no idea how to go about finding an orgy, let alone joining one. And I imagined myself bold until it came time to actually follow through, then I would have a change of heart and slink quietly back out and go eat my feelings in the form of fried seafood, alone, at some fish shack overlooking the bay.

I realized as I lay there, running my fingers through the sand to either side of me, that this was not a good idea, this whole reliving that mythic weekend in Myrtle Beach in 1986. Scott had probably only agreed to come because I proposed Provincetown, and he pictured himself naked and surrounded by men all weekend, drunk on fruity cocktails and sex, with me nowhere around. Like countless other times in my life, I felt like a fool, and I was glad there was no one there to witness it. I decided I would immerse myself in the history of Provincetown, eat a lot of seafood, drink a lot of beer, lie on the beach, and leave when the weekend was over. I'd wave to Scott when I saw him, I guessed, and he'd pay me his share of the rental on the cottage, and we'd part ways. I would fly back to Atlanta and he to Chicago and that was probably going to be it for our friendship—or whatever it was we'd had for twenty-five years.

He was gone when I got back to the cottage. I called and it went to voice mail, so I texted him, then futzed around as I waited for him to respond. When he didn't, I took a shower and ran dripping from it to see if he'd returned my call or texted me. There was nothing.

I dried off and got dressed, and while I did I imagined a scene straight off *Melrose Place* where I walked into town and selected some random gay bar where Scott just so happened to be dancing—shirtless, naturally—with a crowd of guys who looked a lot like him. I pretended not to see him and went to the bar for a drink. The bartender flirted with me and gave me free drinks, then the guys on either side of me started flirting with me and in the mirror behind the bar (because there is always a mirror behind the bar in these scenes) I caught Scott noticing all the attention I was getting, so I threw myself into flirting back and throwing my head back and laughing hysterically at the things all these guys were telling me, even if it wasn't funny. Finally Scott came over and asked how long I'd been there, so I lied and told him I just got there (though, by this time in my fantasy, it had been hours and hours). "I didn't see you," I told him. "Have you been here long?" He was visibly miffed, but I kept going and introduced him to the small crowd of admirers who had gathered around me, all of them hotter than him or the guys he was dancing with. In my fantasy they had names like Cutter and Riley and Jackson, porn star names, and they looked like porn stars, only hotter, and it infuriated Scott. Even in the pulsing lights of the bar—blue, green, purple, blue, green, purple—I could see he turned red with anger. "You can hang out with us if you want," I told him, and glanced around for a seat, but there weren't any because I had so many hot guys clamoring for my attention. "You'll have to stand, though." And I shrugged and that seemed to do it. Scott stalked off, back to his shirtless buddies, and I sat and gloated in my make-believe gay bar with my make-believe admirers.

In reality, though, I just found the nearest restaurant with the best view of the bay and got a seat at the bar where I ate fried clams and drank beer alone. The bartender gave me the most perfunctory of service, I assumed because I didn't act very inviting. I certainly didn't make any attempt to chat him up. Instead, I kept checking my phone to see if Scott had called or texted, and of course he had done neither.

I alternated between wanting to get so drunk I had to crawl back to the cottage and telling myself to just go find some reruns of *The Golden Girls,* stay up late, and sleep in tomorrow. Of course the bartender had to do his job and ask if I wanted another, and I was just about to tell him no, that I was ready to close out, but the guy sitting two seats away spoke up.

103

"Mind if I buy your next one?" I was so startled I could only nod.

I'd noticed him when he sat down, but didn't bother to flirt. He was roughly the size of a Mack truck with a full, black lumberjack beard and a Winnie-The-Pooh t-shirt. When he smiled I thought I saw dimples. He extended a hand. "I'm Andy." That hand was big and soft and I marveled at the way it engulfed mine.

"Mark," I said when I had recovered from my initial shock of having a cute guy buy me a beer.

We talked. He was from Texas and had driven up with friends, but they were only interested in finding men to have sex with, so he'd left them downtown at one of the gay bars. I told him about Scott, and he thought it would be funny if one of his friends ended up tricking with Scott, and we laughed about it. His voice was deep and his drawl pronounced and I was completely smitten. I couldn't tell if his eyes were blue or green, but finding out became important.

After we closed out, we went for a walk on the beach. He told me he'd just broken up with his boyfriend—I was so glad he didn't use the word *partner;* it always sounded more like business than a relationship—after five years, and he'd come to Provincetown to clear his head. "I should have come alone," he said, and looked down at our bare feet in the sand.

"I've been thinking the same thing all day," I confessed. We passed the cottage and I nodded to it.

"That's where I'm staying." It was dark except for the lights on the patio. Scott still wasn't home.

"Fancy," he said. "We're all crammed into two rooms at an inn downtown."

I pitied him. At least I could shut myself in my own room and close the door if I got tired of Scott. The only way Andy could escape was to leave altogether and run the risk of returning at an inconvenient time should one of his friends—there were four of them besides himself—be entertaining a gentleman caller, as he put it with a grin, and I finally saw that he did, in fact, have dimples.

He stayed the night, and I alternated between tiny bouts of panic that Scott would come home and find me with a guy, and hope that he actually would. In the morning we slept late, then showered together, and went in search of breakfast. We went to the beach, then went for lunch—lobster rolls—then back to the cottage. I saw signs that Scott had been there and left again. They seemed deliberate—shoes in the middle of the floor, a tank top thrown across the dining room table when he could just as easily have thrown it into his room.

Andy must have noticed my scowl. "Everything alright?"

"Yeah." We showered together, had sex, napped, then went for dinner. I hinted that he might as well stay the night again, just go get his things and bring them over. He chuckled, but I was being serious, so he said he would and we separated. I went back to the cottage to wait for him and ended up pacing, certain I would never see or hear from him again. He had made his escape. I had assumed too much, grabbed on too tight; he was here with friends, to have fun, not get tied down with one guy when he could have his pick of a thousand others.

He did come back, though. I checked the time and it had been forty minutes; it had just felt like hours. He had a duffel bag and he was smiling. I had never felt such relief in my entire life, but I played it cool. I didn't want him to know how important it was to me that he'd come back.

We had sex and talked while we watched TV with the sound off. He told me he was a chef with a big restaurant group in Houston, and he perked up when I told him I was an attorney. Everyone did. "It's just estate law, though," I explained, quickly. "Nothing flashy."

"Sounds pretty flashy to someone who stands over a stove for a living," he said.

We slept, spooned together. I awoke at some point, certain I had heard my name. I sat up and listened, but there was nothing but the sound of the bay outside and Andy's gentle snores. And maybe I heard something that sounded like footsteps outside the bedroom door, but I couldn't be sure.

Andy stirred. "What...?" he asked, his voice thick with sleep.

"Nothing," I said, and he pulled me back down, wrapped his big arm around me and pulled me to him.

106

That was my weekend: waking up with Andy, showering together, going in search of food, hitting the beach. We took a tour of the island and learned its history, we parasailed, we shopped. Every night we ended up back at the cottage in my bed. Scott came and went when we weren't looking, it seemed. I would be awake, unable to sleep, Andy curled up beside me when I would hear movement on the other side of the bedroom door. I'd slip from under Andy's arm, fumble into my underwear, and go to, I thought, confront Scott. But he had vanished by the time I made it out of the bedroom, like a ghost, leaving only the slightest trace that he was there: a slight drip from the kitchen faucet, the toilet refilling itself.

I felt shame and relief at the same time. On the one hand, I felt I should have tried harder to catch him and make plans and spend some time with him; on the other, I was glad we were avoiding each other. It allowed me to spend as much time with Andy as I could without suffering Scott's scorn or feeling I needed to explain anything. Andy was that boyfriend I had always wanted—that, I admit, I had imagined Scott would be when we would finally declare our love for one another: he was my physical type, he was employed, he laughed a lot, he didn't seek anyone's approval. It was just my luck I would meet the perfect guy on vacation, have five bliss-filled days with him, then say goodbye and never see him again.

"We'll keep in touch," he said, and seemed very sure of it.

I was less sure, but I didn't speak it aloud, lest it manifest itself immediately.

I wondered what relocating to Houston would involve, but I kept it to myself. We had one more day together and I didn't want to scare him away.

I was in a funk the morning of my last day in Provincetown. Andy kept telling me to cheer up, and I tried, but kept falling just short of the mark.

He left first, and I asked if he wanted me to see him off at the ferry, but he said that wouldn't be necessary. I took that to mean he was done with me; vacation was over. He would board the ferry for Boston, catch his plane, fly back to Houston and maybe he would think of me every now and then, but there would be other vacations—for both of us—where we met other guys and fell into pretend relationships for a few days. That was what happened when vacations ended.

So we said goodbye on the street outside the cottage and I went inside to pack. I was sitting on the patio drinking a beer and staring at the bay when Scott showed up to pack. "Your friend gone?" he asked, and I sensed his disapproval, but I was in no mood to argue.

"Yeah, he left about an hour ago," was all I said.

"When's your flight?" he asked me.

"Later tonight," I said. "You heading out now?"

"Plane leaves in a couple hours." He looked rough, like he'd slept in his clothes and there were dark circles under his eyes. I wondered how I'd ever thought him attractive. "I'm going to take a shower and pack," he told me.

He looked better when he emerged later, but some switch in my brain had been flipped and I doubted I would ever look at him the same as before. Instead of relief, I felt sadness, but maybe it was just because I wanted a few more days in Provincetown, with Andy, and that was making me feel differently about Scott.

"Hey, I put the money for my share of the house on the table," he said.

I gave him a wan smile. "Thanks."

He studied me, his brow furrowed. "You okay, Mark?"

"Yeah," I said, but I said it too quickly, so I'm sure it wasn't convincing. "Just bummed to be leaving Provincetown. I could stay here for the rest of my life." *With Andy*, I thought, but did not add.

Scott grinned. "Me, too. Men in Chicago are *nothing* like this!" And he threw me a wink.

I walked him to the door and we hugged and then he was gone. I took one last walk along the beach, checked through the cottage to make sure we weren't leaving a mess, then grabbed my suitcase and started for the ferry. My phone buzzed and when I checked it there was a text from Andy.

Miss U already, it read, with a frowny face emoji. I felt a little better.

That was five years ago. I sent a few texts and Scott responded to them—not always immediately, but he did respond—until he stopped responding and I stopped sending any more. There are relationships that end dramatically, noisily; ours just slowly ceased to exist and neither of us did anything to stop its deterioration. It wasn't a conscious decision on my part, and I couldn't speak for Scott, but one day I realized it had been months—a year, almost—since I'd had any type of contact with him. But even then I didn't do anything to correct it. I didn't call or text or email. Then again, neither did Scott.

Andy texted, though. And he called, albeit drunk. He was coming to Atlanta for work and he wanted to see me. I was thrilled and agreed to everything: yes, I would drive to his hotel at the airport for the sole purpose of seeing him; no, it wasn't out of my way at all; yes, I could make Friday work, no problem. I heard the desperation in my voice, did he? If he did, he made no indication. He just laughed and I pictured his dimples. He would call me a couple days out, he told me, and he did. We confirmed our plans: dinner and drinks at 8 o'clock at his hotel. There was no innuendo, but I couldn't imagine us getting together again—it was over a year since our time together in Provincetown—and not having sex.

But when the weekend rolled around and I didn't hear from him when he'd landed or when he'd checked into his room, I knew he'd changed his mind, or something. I sent him a text and he didn't respond to it until after midnight and said he would hit me up tomorrow. I didn't bother telling him it was okay; I just didn't respond at all. And anyway, he didn't get in touch that next day, either.

Now I'm waiting for Scott to call me and it's been a week already.

He was probably thinking there was no point, because that's what I was thinking. Our friendship had survived my declaration of love for him but had slowly eroded until that weekend in Provincetown. In my mind I likened it to the erosion of glaciers: it was so subtle and the changes so minute that you weren't really aware of it, until a huge chunk of the glacier broke off and thundered into the sea. What would we talk about? I wondered. Or would it be one of those phone calls heavy on awkward silences, broken only occasionally by actual talk, and that of questionable relevance.

Then he did call, and of course I was at the office in a meeting, so I had to send it to voice mail and sit through the remainder of the meeting wondering if he would be pissed off at me because I hadn't accepted his call and would he even bother to answer when I called him back.

When I called him back, he was laughing when he answered. "Mark! What the hell's going on?"

I wasn't exactly sure how to respond, but I was certain he could have been a little more apologetic. "Um... Hi, Scott. I saw you called, so..." If he could act like he hadn't spent the last week intentionally not calling me, then I could pretend I hadn't been waiting.

Scott just laughed. "Yeah, Mom said she saw you," he told me, "and I've been meaning to call, but I've been *so busy.*"

I said nothing, just nodded.

"You still there?" he asked, suddenly. His tone was serious suddenly, like he might actually be concerned that I wasn't.

"I'm here," I said, and stared out my office window at Midtown Atlanta in the rain.

"Well, we need to get together! It's been *ages!*" I recognized this voice as the same voice he used when he sashayed around gay bars.

"Five years," I said.

"Yeah, yeah, yeah," he said, and I hated when people responded like that, dismissively. "So, what are you doing tonight? We could do drinks and dinner... or whatever..."

In my mind, I came up with a litany of excuses why we couldn't get together, from really plausible lies like, "Oh, man... tonight's not good. I have a date," to "I can't tonight, I'm flying out early in the morning for work." I ran through them all in a matter of seconds and rejected each one. The truth was, I wanted to see Scott and tonight was probably going to be the only chance I got to do that. I just wanted him to apologize for keeping me waiting like this for a whole week while he made up his mind to call.

"Yeah," I said, finally. "What time?"

"Eight?" he asked, and I agreed. "You can come pick me up and we can hit The Vortex? I've been craving a good burger."

"The Vortex is good," I said, and outside it rained to match my mood. I should have been glad to finally talk to him, but I wasn't, and knowing I would see him later was already starting to fill me with a mild dread.

Tovah lived in the same house Scott had grown up in. I parked on the street and marveled that not a single thing had changed about the place since the last time I'd seen it, at the shivah for Scott's dad. I rang the doorbell and felt a lurch of panic in my gut as I waited, rocking on my feet, taking note of everything around me: the welcome mat, the door knocker shaped like a pineapple, the mezuzah to the right. Tovah finally answered and beamed up at me. "Mark! So good to see you again!" She held the door open and just before I stepped in, I felt compelled to touch the mezuzah and kiss my fingers.

"How are you, Tovah?"

"I'm good! Come in, come in. Scott's still getting ready." I followed her through the dark foyer and into the living room where a rerun of *Matlock* played on a television set I am certain was there when I would visit in high school. "Can I get you something to drink?"

"Oh, I'm fine. Thanks."

"Well, I'm having wine," she said, and threw me an exaggerated wink over her shoulder as she disappeared around a corner and into the kitchen.

I stood where I was, a time traveler, surrounded by chintz and wicker and wallpaper over wainscoting. Then my eye was drawn to the wall where Tovah had hung Scott's senior picture from high school. I stared hard at it and felt such a piercing sadness that I actually grabbed my chest where it hurt. He had been one of the most beautiful men I'd ever known in my life and the portrait captured everything that made him that so well: the hair so red it almost seemed unreal, and the blue eyes under a straight brow line; the nose that he didn't get from either Tovah or his father; the line of his jaw, the width of his shoulders.

Being older—wiser—now, I looked at that face and understood why he and I could never have been anything more than friends. Then there were his football and basketball and baseball photos arranged around it, in case it weren't clear enough to me. I would have laughed were it not for that ache of sadness.

Tovah rescued me from my emotions by rounding the corner, a bottle of wine in one hand and a corkscrew in the other. "Mark, would you be a dear and help an old lady out? This thing is giving me fits."

"Sure," I said.

I was in the process of working the partly broken cork out of the bottle when Scott came down the stairs. The sight of him almost caused me to drop the bottle, and I audibly gasped.

"Hey, stranger," he said, and swept me into a hug.

"Hey," I said, and did my best to return the embrace with as much fervor as it was being given. I searched my brain for something more to say, anything really, but seeing him—and like this—had wiped my thoughts clean, except for one. *He's sick.* Because even now, decades after the crisis was at its zenith, and in an age when new drugs allowed people to live longer and healthier lives without even the risk of transmitting the virus to their partners, I was stuck on the term we used back then: sick. Like Tovah's furniture and wallpaper, my vocabulary for the disease had not made it out of the early Nineties.

"You look good, Mark."

And I lied and said, "You, too!" He did not look good. He didn't look bad, necessarily, and I had certainly seen people look worse, but he didn't look healthy. He was thinner than I had ever seen him, there were dark circles around his eyes, and his cheeks were sunken. His hair was thinning and that glorious copper had faded to a mousy brown. I felt like crying, and when I turned away from Scott, before he could catch it on my face, I caught Tovah studying me.

She was not smiling and she looked depleted. She recovered, and in another second, she was laughing as she poured herself a glass of wine, having successfully completed the extraction of the broken cork from her bottle. "So, where you boys going tonight? What are you going to do? I'm sure you have a lot to catch up on!"

Scott and I both shrugged. "We'll play it by ear, I guess," I said, sufficiently recovered from my initial shock at his appearance.

"Well, I'm starving," he said, and it caused Tovah and I both to look away again.

He grabbed a jacket off the hall tree—brass, and polished to a sheen as fresh as twenty-five years ago—and we started out. "Goodbye, Tovah," I said.

She ran after us, her wine sloshing. "You boys be safe!" she said, and Scott laughed. I was about to laugh, too; it sounded so theatrical. We were going to Midtown Atlanta, not a Third World country in revolt. But the desperation in her face made me catch myself. She gripped my arm. Scott was already out the door and she couldn't reach him. Or maybe she knew it was too late for him, but I might be convinced still. "Have fun," she said, "but *be safe.*"

I nodded. "I'll look after him, Tovah."

Her lips tightened into what would have to do for a smile and she nodded, let go of my arm. "You got your key, Scotty?"

"Yes, Mom."

"Okay, you boys have fun."

She and I shared one last long look as she closed the door, locked it behind us. Scott was already halfway to my car and I took a quick opportunity to collect myself, fix my face. *She knows,* I told myself, and I wasn't sure how, because I was certain that Scott still hadn't come out to her, but she knew. Mothers always knew, I supposed.

"You coming?" Scott called to me.

"Yeah," I said. "I was just going over everything at home, making sure I turned everything off and locked the door." It was a weak lie, but it would have to do.

I drove us into Midtown in silence. Scott chattered like a toddler, about how different everything was since he'd last seen Atlanta. "And people are moving back into town from the suburbs?" He found that unbelievable. Then he asked me, "Are you okay?"

"I'm fine. Why?"

"I think I'm getting a headache."

"Oh. Well, take something, girl! I can't have you moping around all night!"

At The Vortex we got a table and I concentrated on the menu to keep from staring at him. It was dark in the restaurant and I was glad for that. "I'm getting the biggest burger they have," he declared, and when our server came he did just that. "And a vodka and cranberry."

I ordered a basic cheeseburger and a beer, and the server took the menus so I couldn't not look at Scott. I smiled to hide my shock. "So... how have you been?" Small talk. I knew very well how he had been: he was sick. I didn't want to jump to any conclusions on my own, but I didn't really know how to ask him about his health, either.

He shrugged. "You know... working too much, not getting paid enough. The usual. You're looking good, though, Mark. You been working out?"

I just gave him a withering look. He knew as well as I did that I had not been working out. I hovered around one-eighty, give or take five pounds. I wore it well and hid it with clothes. "No," I said simply.

He fired a round of questions at me. Was I seeing anyone? Well, why not? Was I just tricking around, then? He laughed when I asked him if he had ever known me to trick around like that. How was work going? Had I made partner yet?

Our drinks came and it was my turn to ask the questions. How was work? Was he seeing anyone? "I'm seeing a few people," he said, laughing. I couldn't even pretend to find it funny. He looked like he had lost some weight, I pointed out—was everything okay? I didn't believe he would answer me honestly, and he didn't. "I've just been working a buttload of hours," he explained with a shrug. "You know how it is." I told him I did; what I didn't tell him was that when I worked a lot of overtime on a case, I didn't look ill.

I knew that Scott knew he was sick, too, and I also knew that he had not gotten tested to be certain. And he never would. I knew guys like that. On hookup sites they put their status as "Don't Know" or they outright lied and said they were negative, or at the very least they claimed they were undetectable, but one look at them and it was clear they were anything but. It infuriated me and it broke my heart and I tried to ignore those emotions and just drink my beer, but they welled up in me and I had to excuse myself to go to the bathroom.

"I'll be here," Scott said, and I fled to the men's room.

I locked myself in a stall and fought back tears. I felt defeated, as if I had failed without ever having a chance. Scott was sick and I had failed. I could have kept this from happening, I felt, if he had only let me. For years I had held on to the prospect that he and I would, eventually, get together, that he'd look at me and see that I was the one person who had always been there, the only real constant in his life. Waiting for him had kept me from pursuing other possibilities, at least seriously. I felt beaten and dejected, then resentment, at myself and at Scott. For thirty years, this had been my whole life: waiting for Scott to see me and want me, and now all that was over and I didn't know what the next step was.

I lost track of time as I sat there, the music blaring for some reason. A guy came in, talked loudly on his cell phone as he peed. I expected Scott to come for me, but he didn't. Finally I stood, flushed in case anyone was there and might think it strange for someone to emerge from a bathroom stall without doing so, and washed my hands. I fished my phone out of my pocket and checked the time—only six minutes had elapsed. I was certain I'd been sitting there for an hour, at least.

Scott was unconcerned when I returned to the table. The food had been delivered and he was halfway through his burger already. "It's getting cold," he told me.

"I'm actually not as hungry as I thought I was," I said.

He shrugged and continued to eat. I sat in silence as he finished his burger and fries and ordered another drink—his third. My beer had gotten warm, but I drank it anyway. It did little to drown the hot ball of despair that had settled in my gut. I just wanted to go home. This was a bad idea and that was the only way I could think to deal with it, to just escape.

Scott would have none of that, though. "So, let's hit Blake's," he suggested.

"I don't know..."

He scowled. "Oh, come on. We haven't seen each other in five years, Mark. The least you could do is hang out with me for more than an hour."

Of course I relented. The server asked if there was something wrong with my burger. It still sat, untouched, and I told her it was fine, I just wasn't hungry. No, I didn't need to box it up. She shrugged, dropped the check, and walked away.

"It's on me," Scott said, and looked as if he expected me to argue. I didn't. It just didn't matter to me.

We left and since it was a nice night out, Scott suggested we walk to Blake's. I didn't argue that, either, though it was chilly and driving would have taken all of three minutes. So we walked, me with my hands crammed into my pockets and Scott sashaying before me as if everyone walking or driving by was doing so just to get a glimpse of him. So much had changed about him, but that never would, I guessed.

I searched my memory for some pivotal moment in our lives together when things had gone off the rails. I could still see him on that first day we met thirty years ago, stuffed into the back of that van bound for the beach. He had been the superlative example of manhood to me then, everything I would never be but that I secretly hoped to find in a partner when I was older, out on my own and more comfortable with my own sexuality. For years, even as I watched him priss around gay bars, he had remained my ideal; even when he rejected me so roundly in the wake of my declaration of love. Had that been it? No, because I still held out hope that at some point he would realize what he could have with me and want it as much as I did.

But maybe it had just slowly eroded, like his façade of masculinity. Maybe this is what he had always wanted to be, like I had always wanted him, and we had just wanted two very different things. His was achievable; mine was doomed to fail.

"Catch up," he said, and I snapped out of my reverie to see he was a good ten feet ahead of me, standing with his arms akimbo the way my mother would when she scolded me as a child. "What's wrong?" he asked when I caught up with him.

"What do you mean?" I asked him, and only barely glanced at him.

"You had a weird look on your face there for a minute," he explained. "You looked like you'd seen a ghost."

Maybe I did, I thought, and we waited together for the light to change so we could cross Peachtree.

In Mysterious Ways

The man jumped from the top floor of the Westin's parking deck downtown just after two o'clock on Tuesday afternoon. He hadn't considered this in the weeks before, but had he done it earlier or later in the day, there would have been more people on the sidewalk and someone else might have been crushed. As it turned out, he was the only casualty.

Later, at six and eleven, it would be on the news and people—none of them actual witnesses—would be perplexed. They would say they hadn't known this man, or why he did it. They would wonder aloud why, their eyes wide from the shock of this thing they hadn't seen. They would look into the camera and say what a terrible thing it was for a man to jump to his death from the top of a parking deck. One of them would wonder *What if a child had seen?* On TV, it is always good to mention the potential devastating effects an incident might have on a child. Those responsible for the news believed this was important, as it created interest. No one bothered to consider the foolishness of it, because there were no children present when the man jumped.

There were two actual witnesses: a young woman from Mexico with the name of a famous American singer, and a black man with a Spanish name. The man hit the sidewalk between them. In the second after it happened, they looked first at this thing that had made such a noise when it fell from the sky and saw that it was a man—or, rather, what remained of a man—the blood already pooling around him and seeping from his mouth, his nostrils, and his wide-open eyes, which were green; then they looked at each other, one's shock evident to the other. Her name was Diana. His was Alfredo.

The black man, who was tall and quick and did not think, leaped over the crushed body, put himself between the woman and the dead man, said, "It's okay. Don't look. Just don't look."

She looked anyway and saw, just as her vision blurred and she felt herself passing out in the arms of this man whose name she would never know, something gather in the air above the crushed corpse: the man's soul, or his ghost, his *fantasma*. Around her, people screamed as they realized what had happened. Diana did not scream. She was not afraid. She knew about death.

When she was five, her father, in a rage, shot and killed her mother. He believed Diana's mother was sleeping with a man named Fernando. Diana's father was waiting when her mother came home from somewhere. He yelled at her and she yelled back and he shot her with a gun he had bought just three days earlier. Then, sobbing and frantic, he aimed the pistol into his mouth and pulled the trigger. Diana found them, her father's body having fallen across her mother's, their blood mingling and spreading beneath them. Diana was terrified and confused, but she ran the five kilometers to the house of her *tía*, screaming that someone had killed her mother and father. When she was older she understood that her father was the killer. No one told her outright, but she knew from the things they said. This was how she learned about death.

"Sit here. It's okay." The black man led her to a bench where, before the man jumped to his death, people waited for the bus. Those people were on their feet now, asking what happened and craning their necks to see.

Diana wondered if they, too, had seen the man's soul leave his body there on the sidewalk. She wouldn't look again. She knew the soul or ghost or whatever was gone now. These people wanted to see the body, the blood, not the man's spirit. When the bus came a few moments later, she boarded it and sat in the back where she could not see the body or the crowd of people gathering around it. That night, she would dream she was standing outside the hotel where she had applied for a job as a housekeeper, and that as she waited to cross the street a young man with green eyes and a yellow tie would step alongside her. She would smile and he would smile, and Diana would know that he was better where he was now.

When the police arrived, and after them the news teams, Alfredo told them there had been a woman. "She was standing with me when he fell," he told them, but that woman was nowhere to be seen, so they did not care about her. They asked him what he had seen, how it had happened, and he told them. He had shaved that morning with a dull razor and he scratched his chin as he spoke, first to the officers and then to the reporter, who was Asian and wore perfume. "I was just standing there, and he fell. Just like that. WHUMP! You know?" He felt the need to make it clear he had nothing to do with it. "I didn't know him and I don't know why he did it." The pretty Asian reporter asked what he'd thought when it happened and Alfredo said that he was just glad no children had seen it. This will be on the news later, Alfredo scratching his chin and saying this.

He would worry for weeks about why, of all the people who could have been standing on the sidewalk when this man he will never know jumped from the parking deck, it had to be him. People he knew said the Lord tested people and he guessed this was a test, because he wasn't supposed to be there at that time, on Tuesday afternoon. He should have been working, but he had quit his job over the weekend. He was tired of washing dishes for a living. He had decided he was too old to wash dishes. He would find something else to do that paid more and was not so demeaning.

His ex-wife would be furious. She would want the child support. Already she wanted more than he could pay and she was always threatening him: she would take him to court, she would not let him see the kids, she would call her brothers and they would deal with him. He would remind her that she was the one who told him to find something else, that a forty-four-year-old man should do more than wash dishes, that he should be ashamed of himself. He would tell her that, but she would still be angry.

"The good Lord works in mysterious ways," Alfredo's mother, who was very devout, would say. "He wants you to learn something from washing dishes." She was not ashamed of him.

"What He want me to learn, then?" Alfredo asked. He was not as devout as his mother.

"That's between you and Him."

126

Alfredo guessed he had learned all he needed: that a man his age with three grown children by one woman and two more by the woman who now hated him so needed a better job. He wasn't sure what this other thing meant. What was to be learned witnessing a man half his age jumping to his death?

"Everything happens for a reason." His mother said this a lot, but Alfredo was not so sure. He could find no sense in it. He sat in his apartment—a motel room, really; he rented by the week—that night after watching himself on the news and wondered if he'd imagined the young woman. He was drinking beer he couldn't afford and his neck and chin still itched from that dull razor, and he wondered if he'd imagined her. He could remember the face of the dead man: he'd had green eyes and black hair and his tie was yellow. Alfredo remembered how the blood came out of his eyes and nostrils and mouth, like a slow-motion replay on TV. But he could remember nothing about the young woman, as if she hadn't been there at all.

Diana told no one. She didn't want to talk about it because she wasn't sure how to say that she'd watched a man die, then his soul leave his body. She didn't want people to think she was crazy. She did not watch the news. She didn't want to be reminded. She knew enough about death.

Four months ago, she used all the money she had saved, and planned to send her *tía*, to get an abortion. She didn't need another child. Her boyfriend agreed; neither of them needed this responsibility. She had a son and a daughter, living with her aunt in Mexico; he had none and didn't want any. He drove her to the clinic, waited outside in his car, smoking cigarettes and listening to Los Tigres del Norte and talking on his cell phone to another girl, who was younger and prettier than Diana. Afterward, he drove her back to her apartment. They did not speak of what they had done, like in a movie when two people murder someone and bury the body and never discuss it. A week later, when he called to tell her he was seeing someone else, she was not surprised.

In her dreams, that baby was a boy with green eyes and he could fly. *"¡Mírame, mami—puedo volar!"*

"Sí. Te veo."

In that dream, she called him Michael, but she didn't know why. Perhaps, like herself, after a famous American singer.

Alfredo found it odd, when he thought about it, that he saw so little of his three grown children. One daughter lived in California where it never got cold. She was the eldest. A son lived in Chicago, which was nothing like California. The other son, the youngest of the three, lived in Atlanta, but Alfredo never saw him. They never spoke on the phone and—this surprised Alfredo—they never passed one another on the street. This son visited Alfredo's mother often, and she was his source of news about this son: he'd graduated high school, he'd graduated college, he was a graphic designer, he was a homosexual.

Alfredo knew where his son worked, and where he lived, but he never called and never visited. He told people that he was ashamed of his gay son; what he never said was that he was more ashamed of himself. What son wanted anything to do with a father who washed dishes for a living and drank beer he couldn't afford, alone in his motel apartment with all the lights off?

When this son was born, Alfredo wanted to name him after himself, but his wife wouldn't hear of it. The child needed his own name, she said, and named him Deon, which Alfredo hadn't liked because it sounded too much like a woman's name. When this son was older, he went to an attorney and changed his name, and now he was William. Alfredo liked that better, even if it wasn't his own name.

After watching the man die on the sidewalk, Alfredo thought he might call his son. Being close to death made people do things like that. It made them want to get closer to the people in their lives because it became clear that anything could happen. Alfredo was worried something might happen, but he wasn't sure what it might be. Still, though, he did not call. He asked his mother and she said that his son was doing just fine.

Two days after the man with green eyes jumped to his death, a woman from that hotel called Diana to schedule an interview, and could she come the following Monday at ten a.m.? Diana thanked the woman, whose name she would not remember. She said she would be there on Monday.

She rode the bus, then the train, where she sat beside a man her mother had loved. Diana didn't know this, though he smiled at her and said, *"Hola."* She smiled back and said, *"Hola."* They didn't speak again. The man who had loved her mother spoke in whispers to a young black man who was with him, but they spoke English and Diana didn't understand what they said.

The train stopped. Diana got off and rode the escalator up and walked to the hotel. There was nothing where the man had fallen the week before. It was like it had never happened. No one stopped to point and say "Here. This is where he fell when he jumped."

She didn't notice, but the young black man and the man her mother had loved had left the train station after her. She walked into the hotel and didn't look back to where they stopped on the sidewalk, first looking up at the dizzying height of the building, then down at the place on the sidewalk, where now there was nothing.

"It was here?" asked the man, whose name was Fernando. He had flown in from Texas to bury his son, who had jumped to his death from the top floor of the parking deck of this famous hotel. He was tired and anguished.

"Yes," said the younger man. His name was William.

Fernando stood silent, his eyes closed. He stood like that for a long time. People walked around him, did not notice the man or his misery. He opened his eyes finally and gave William, who had been his son's lover, a weak smile. "Thank you. We can go now."

They walked back to the train station and rode the escalator down, boarded the next train, and went north. They didn't speak. Later that afternoon, Fernando returned to Texas on a plane full of people who had no idea he had buried his youngest son, Miguel—who preferred, when he was a man, to be called Michael.

He closed his eyes and remembered the face of a woman he had loved years ago who was long dead, thought how very much she had resembled the young woman on the train that morning. And he thought of his son.

When he was little, four years old, Miguel tied a yellow towel around his neck like it was a cape and climbed onto the bed of his father's old pickup truck.

"¡Mírame, papi—puedo volar!"

"Sí. Te veo!" Fernando had laughed, but even at that height, a tiny boy could hurt himself. *"Pero... ten cuidado, hijo."*

Miguel had laughed. *"¡Voy a volar!"* And he went up on the tips of his toes, spread his arms. The wind caught the towel that was his superhero's cape, and for an instant it was like he was actually flying.

Black Is the Color of My True Love's Hair

It has been six months since Philip nearly died when a woman, distracted by her cell phone, drove through a traffic light and plowed into him. Howard hasn't been marking the days, not like that—with big, red X's on a calendar or anything—but he is reminded of it when he gets a text from the guy he was having sex with when it happened.

Hey, this new text says, and above it, the last text from the same guy, with the date and time it was sent. Six months ago, to the day. *That was fun*, says that text, and it makes Howard sick. He considers replying, lying and telling the guy he has the wrong number. Honestly, he wouldn't even remember the guy's name if he hadn't entered it into his phone. *Dave*. He has only a vague recollection of what Dave looks like, anyway, and what he remembers isn't enough to make him respond. He decides to just ignore it.

Philip has been home for three months. His improvement has been slow but steady. The injury to his brain affected his memory, so he didn't remember the wreck; he didn't even seem to want to talk about it, and Howard was glad for that. It has impaired his speech, too, but that doesn't keep him from asking Howard a litany of questions on a daily basis. "How long was I in the... coma?" His speech is halting, he has to search for some words, or Howard has to provide them.

"Two weeks," Howard tells him.

They are having dinner. Howard has grilled steaks and Philip insists on cutting his own. They sit at TV tray tables in the living room and Philip slices at his ribeye like he is sawing a log, his lips in a tight line, his face set. Howard watches, nervous, ready to leap in should the situation become critical and the meat slide to the floor.

"I can do it," Philip says, through his teeth.

"Okay," Howard says, though he is beginning to doubt.

"Stop... staring like that." There are tears welling in Philip's eyes, but he doesn't stop trying to cut the steak. Howard can't take it. He puts his hand on Philip's, takes the knife, and steps in.

"Let me do it." He says it gently, just barely above a whisper.

Philip stares hard at a point somewhere past Howard as the tears roll down his cheeks. He says nothing, so Howard cuts the steak into more manageable pieces and fights the urge to cry himself. It's hard on Philip, always so self-sufficient before, but it's hard on Howard, too. Not helping him do the things that came so easily before, but knowing that he couldn't have done anything to prevent the accident that left Philip so helpless, and knowing that when it happened, he'd been fucking a total stranger in a hotel.

Howard got the call as he was pulling into the driveway. It was sunny that day, with one of those skies so blue it was hard to believe. He'd left the hotel in Buckhead and made it back to the Highlands without hitting any of the rush hour traffic, so he was in a good mood. He thought he might hit the gym.

He noticed Phillip's car wasn't in the driveway, and that was odd—Phillip always beat him home in the afternoons. Maybe he'd gone for a drink with friends after work. Howard checked his phone, but there were no messages from Philip. There was one from Dave, though, the guy he'd just had sex with. *That was fun*, it read, and Howard smiled. It had been fun. He would reply to it later. Maybe they could get together again while Dave was in town.

He'd just started typing out a message to Philip, to tell him he was going to the gym in case Philip got home and wondered where he was, when an incoming call interrupted it. Normally, Howard would ignore it and let it go to voice mail, but he answered this one. People always said they "just had a feeling" when they answered the phone and it was bad news, but he could not say why he answered that call. Maybe because he was annoyed it had interrupted his text. Maybe because he meant to reject the call and answered it instead. He honestly couldn't say.

"Howard Koren?" The voice was firm, authoritative, but not rude.

"Yes...?"

"There's been an accident. We have your name as the emergency contact for Philip Duncan..."

Howard sat, paralyzed by shock, as the voice gave him the necessary details: there had been an accident, Philip was injured, he was treated at the scene, then airlifted to Grady Hospital. "He's alive?" Howard asked, and even to himself his voice sounded like it was coming out of a barrel.

"I honestly can't answer that question," said the man, matter-of-factly. "I don't have that information. I'm sorry."

Howard wondered what it must be like to have this job where you call people to give them horrific news, then tell them you don't have all the information if they started asking questions. He thought he might be angry, but it died just as quick as it flared up, and he said only, "Thank you for calling," then ended the call and backed out of the driveway, a cocktail of emotions swirling through him and landing in the pit of his stomach, where they felt a lot like disgust. He knew he should be terrified, and maybe that would come as he made his way through traffic to the trauma center at Grady, but right then all he felt was disgust, and it was directed at himself. Because he could still smell Dave and the sex they'd had on himself.

Early in their relationship, Howard would never have considered having sex with anyone other than Philip, and not just for reasons of emotional fidelity. Philip was the exact physical type he had always imagined, so then—they were both in their mid-twenties—he had been monogamous with the ferocity of an activist. Guys his age at work boasted in one breath of their love for their boyfriends, then

135

bragged—albeit in whispers—of the torrid sex they'd had the night before with some guy they cruised in the showers at the gym. "His dick was just so big!" they declared, feigning embarrassment, yet betrayed by their smiles. "I just couldn't help myself!"

"What about your boyfriend, though?" Howard asked, and they shrugged, or waved a hand dismissively.

"Oh, you know. What he doesn't know won't hurt him."

Howard was appalled.

Later he told Philip, who just shrugged. "Some people are like that," was his assessment. "Monogamy just isn't important to them, especially when they're young." He sounded like he wasn't young himself, like he was some seasoned veteran of the war on monogamy dispensing his sage wisdom from a perch high above such trivial concerns.

Howard scoffed. "And they wonder why everyone thinks gays will fuck anything that moves." He tried to go back to reading his book—*Equal Affections* by David Leavitt, which, he would eventually find to his exasperation, also touched on the infidelity inherent in gay relationships—but found it difficult to concentrate on the words. He set it aside and turned to Philip on his side of the bed. "Monogamy's not a problem, is it?" he asked. "With us, I mean..."

Philip actually laughed. "No, sweetie," he said. "Monogamy is not a problem for me."

"Okay, good." Howard turned back to his book and Philip leaned over, kissed his neck just behind his ear, and called him silly.

The longer they were together, though, and the longer they stayed monogamous, it became clear to the two of them that they were in the minority. They sat at parties and in bars and listened as couples spoke of their open relationships in the same tones they spoke of buying new furniture or vacationing in Malta. Chuck and Jerry, who worked with Philip and invited them for dinner, seemed genuinely surprised that two healthy, young males in their prime would limit themselves sexually, so early. "But... you play with other people *together*, right?" Chuck asked.

"No," Howard said, simply. Because it was simple.

"Not even *once?*" Jerry chimed in. They were both in their late forties, fussy and effete; Howard marveled at their attraction to one another. They matched their surroundings—giant floral prints on the furniture, ornate lighting, statuary—perfectly.

"Nope," Philip replied.

"Well, that is just the sweetest thing," Chuck said, but the expression on his face said otherwise.

Jerry was less diplomatic. "You'll grow out of it," he said. "Believe me."

Howard felt his annoyance rising. He didn't have to believe these two condescending, old queens. And if they were so physically disgusted by one another, then why did they even stay together? It made no sense to him, and he mentioned it to Philip when they got home. "If *that* is what I have to look forward to, then just kill me now," he said as he undressed, balling his shirt and socks and throwing them into the hamper like he was lobbing grenades.

"They're good people, though," Philip said from where he sat on the edge of the bed, peeling off his socks and picking at the lint between his toes.

"They're *nice* people," Howard corrected him. "It's not the same."

Philip threw him a look. "Since when are you so judgmental?"

Howard gave a short bark of laughter. "*I'm* judgmental? We just spent three hours being told we're not gay enough because we don't fuck other people, Philip."

"I don't think that's what they were saying..."

"It's exactly what they were saying."

The argument ended the way all their arguments ended: it was there one minute and gone the next and Howard was wrapped around Philip in bed, watching reruns of *The Golden Girls* until he fell asleep with the beat of Philip's heart in his ear.

As he watched Philip recover from the accident—two weeks in a medically-induced coma and two weeks out of it—Howard revisited that discussion and how he'd felt in the wake of Chuck and Jerry's disdain, and how, in the end, it turned out to be more of a prophecy than a judgment. They had grown out of monogamy, as Jerry had said they would, and it had happened with no great revelation or fanfare on either Howard's or Philip's part. It just happened.

Philip brought it up. They were in the car, on the way home from dinner out. It was the best place for a discussion like that, Howard realized; neither of them could excuse himself from it if they didn't like what was being said. "I've been thinking," Philip began, and Howard thought he might be about to suggest Palm Springs for vacation, instead of Hawaii.

"About what?"

"Us," Philip replied, and Howard's stomach dropped.

"What about us?"

Philip chuckled. "I'm not about to break up with you, so you can relax."

Howard tried to laugh, too, but it came out sounding more like a cough. "What, then?"

It started in the car and ended in the kitchen with them facing one another across the island. Howard nursed a beer; Philip sipped wine. Neither raised his voice. "I just feel like I'm losing something," Howard said.

Philip set his wine down, walked around the island, and pulled Howard to him. Never was the difference in their sizes more apparent than when they stood so close. "Don't be silly," he said. "You can't get rid of me that easily."

The truth was that Howard had already slept with someone else—a guy named Jay, from the bank where he worked. They'd gone for drinks after work, then Jay had suggested they head to his place, since it was literally across the street. It had been unexpected and clumsy, and Howard had felt horrible afterwards, upbraiding himself on the drive home. "Idiot," he hissed at himself, and slammed his fist against the steering wheel. Jay wasn't even his type—too short, too stocky, blond—but somehow those things hadn't mattered enough to inspire him to put a stop to Jay's subtle flirting at the bar, or his obvious advances once they got to his apartment.

Now, though, Philip was suggesting they open up the relationship. Not because he was tired of Howard, but because it would actually make sex between them more exciting for its familiarity. Like coming home and sleeping in your own bed after a vacation, as he'd explained it.

"When do you plan to go back to work?" Howard's mother asked him a week after Philip had returned home. Judy Stein prided herself on her attention to practical matters and her directness. They were in the kitchen and Howard was making coffee.

"When Philip can manage on his own, Mom."

"And when will that be?"

Howard knew his mother. She wasn't being a bitch on purpose; it was just her way, as she called it. She was nosy, passive-aggressive, bossy—whatever the situation called for. He'd been dealing with it his entire life. But something about *this* line of questioning, at *this* exact moment, concerning *this* situation made him pause in scooping the coffee into the filter, grip the edge of the counter until his knuckles turned white, and grit his teeth. "Soon," he said, forced it out through his clenched jaw.

"Well, how soon?" Judy seemed genuinely perplexed, her eyes blinking behind her enormous glasses.

"Soon, Mom. Just... *soon*. When Philip can stand up and walk by himself, and go take a shit by himself, and piss without having to sit down and be helped back up." Howard had lost count of how many scoops of coffee he'd added to the percolator. *Fuck it,* he thought, and added one more. Judy would hate it and he was perfectly fine with that. He set it to brew and turned to face his mother. She stared at him, completely nonplussed by his outburst. He continued, regardless: "When he can manage the stairs by himself without falling and breaking his goddamned neck, Mom. I don't know when. Shit! *Soon!*"

"Well, you don't have to yell."

"I'm not yelling!" But he was.

"I just don't want you to lose your job, being gone so long."

Howard rolled his eyes and laughed. "I'm not going to lose my job, Mom. This isn't flipping burgers for minimum wage and no benefits. I'm covered." Not to mention that he checked in regularly every day by both email and phone, but Judy—who had never worked a single day in her entire life—wouldn't understand it, even if he broke it down for her.

"I'll cut the babka," she said, and stood to do so.

"I'll check on Philip."

"Oh, let him sleep," Judy said, as she rummaged through the drawers in search of a knife. Howard reached around her and pulled one from the block on the counter, handed it to her, and went up the back stairs.

Philip lay on his back, his mouth open, a tiny rivulet of saliva dripping down the side of his face. Something in Howard broke every time he came to see that Philip was okay. Maybe it was the guilt, but he suspected it was something much more, he just couldn't name it. Not yet.

They'd shaved Philip's head in the hospital and Howard had burst into tears the first time he'd seen it, that thick mop of black curls reduced to little more than five o'clock shadow interrupted by the white crescent of the scar over the left ear. Philip looked small with no hair, lessened. It was growing back slowly, but it would be months before it returned to its original splendor. Howard took a tissue from the bedside table and dabbed at the saliva, causing Philip to stir.

His eyelids fluttered and it took a second for him to focus on Howard's face. He smiled. "Hey..." His voice was a croak.

"I'm sorry, baby. I didn't mean to wake you."

"Something... wrong?"

Howard stroked the fuzz on his head. "No, baby. You were just drooling a little." He held up the tissue as proof.

Philip made a face, closed his eyes. He was asleep again in less than a second, and Howard noticed his eyelashes. No matter the state of the hair on his head, Philip's lashes were still thick and black as fans.

Interestingly enough, less than a handful of their friends visited the hospital while Philip was in the coma. Chuck and Jerry came, and it caught Howard so off his guard, he was speechless. They bore flowers—an elaborate arrangement of wildly-colored Asiatic lilies and Bird of Paradise—and a teddy bear in workout attire. "You poor thing," Jerry said, and sounded as if he genuinely meant it.

"He's... Philip's in a coma," Howard informed them, once he found his voice, and they nodded because they already knew. "The doctor thought it would reduce the risk of permanent damage to his brain, so they induced it..."

"How are *you*, though?" Chuck asked, and gave Howard's shoulder a matronly squeeze.

Howard considered all the things he might say: good, fine, holding up, taking it one day at a time. All the clichés everyone had memorized and heard a million times. "I'm scared to death," he said, whispered it like a confession.

They clucked and nodded in sympathy, a pair of dowager aunties who had seen it all and could be counted on for strength and practicality in the face of uncertainty. They barraged him with questions: had he eaten? had he slept? was there anything he needed from the store? from home? Howard was rendered speechless again, faced with so much noble generosity. In the end, he surrendered his key so that Chuck and Jerry could take the trash out and bring him a change of clothes, otherwise they might never have left the hospital.

After that first visit, they came once a week and insisted that Howard allow them to do something for him. He relented each time, and when it was time for Philip to be released, they arrived home to a newly mowed lawn and freshly clipped hedges outside, and fresh flowers in every room inside. The house was immaculate, and there was a note. *Welcome home, Philip! Much love to the both of you!—Chuck and Jerry.*

Philip laughed, but at first, Howard wasn't sure what sound he was making. "Is something wrong?" He was reduced to naked panic so easily since the accident.

"See?" Philip asked, grinning. "Good... people."

Other friends and acquaintances called or texted. Howard answered them or he didn't, depending on how important he felt they were, or how serious their concern. He spent the better part of a day updating everyone that mattered. The rest could wait.

Judy had kept her hospital visits to a minimum, but since she lived less than ten minutes from them, in Toco Hills, she drove to Virginia-Highland every other day, at least, and she always had a rational explanation. "I was on my way back from Doris Friedman's," she would explain. "She's sitting shivah, you know. Her husband died, just like that." She snapped her fingers for emphasis. "Heart attack. Out of the blue."

Howard was reminded how close he'd come to sitting shivah himself. The next time, she was on her way to the salon, then she was going to see her doctor and thought she'd run by and see how Philip was. "Mom, you don't need a reason," Howard told her when she said she was on her way to the library. "Just come by. It's okay."

"I don't want to be a bother, Howard," Judy said, and the look on her face hinted at the pain she would surely feel knowing she was a nuisance.

Howard just rolled his eyes.

"Do you need anything?" she asked, whispering. "I'll run out to the grocery for you."

"We're fine. And you don't have to whisper." He led her into the kitchen. "They've got him on so many painkillers, you could drop a bomb and he'd sleep through it." He gathered the makings of coffee.

"He's getting better, though?"

"Yes." Philip was improving, but it was the slowest process Howard had ever witnessed in his life. He'd broken his arm and cracked two ribs falling from a tree at Camp Barney when he was thirteen, and he remembered a few instances of difficulty, but other than that he was whole again by the time school started back in September. Watching Philip heal from such a traumatic brain injury was like watching grass grow, and neither of them were as patient as they needed to be. Howard wanted immediate results, or at least something like when his broken arm and ribs healed completely in four weeks instead of six, like the doctor had said. He wanted daily milestones, adding up to weekly achievements, leading to a complete recovery that would leave the team of physicians at Grady's trauma center speechless. What he got was healing at the pace of a glacier, which frustrated Philip to the point that all he could do was clench his fists and express his irritation with a drawn out grunt through clenched teeth. Howard would usually have to excuse himself from the room; he didn't want Philip to see him cry. He wanted to appear strong, yes, but he feared that, in those moments, something more than weakness might show in his eyes. He was convinced that if he let his guard down for even a second, Philip, Judy, the doctors, Chuck and Jerry, they would all know where he had been and what he was doing, and with a total stranger, when this happened to Philip.

"Sorry....," Philip would tell him, usually at night when they lay in bed before he drifted off to sleep and Howard slipped away to the guest bedroom across the hall. Philip was in so much pain, Howard had decided they would sleep apart until all the broken bones healed at least. "Such a... problem..."

"Shh," Howard said, and squeezed his hand. "You're not a problem. You don't have to apologize." He turned and gave Philip a reassuring smile.

Philip's mouth was working as he searched his malfunctioning brain for the words he wanted to say. "Love...," he finally said, and followed it with a huge sigh that conveyed the effort he had put into it. Sometimes he was able to communicate in fractured sentences; other times, a single word was all he could come up with.

Tears welled in Howard's eyes. He wanted to run from the room, but something held him where he was this time, and he smiled as the tears rolled down his cheeks. "I love you, too, baby," he said, and kissed Philip full on the mouth. It seemed like forever since they had kissed like that.

If anyone had asked him, when he was younger, what he thought his life would be like in his twenties, his thirties, his forties, Howard would have got most of it right. There were no out celebrities when he was coming to terms with his own sexuality, no role models other than drag queens and porn stars, so he based his predictions on those: he would get a loft in the city, he would work out five times a week, he would be tan year-round, he would only date the hottest guys, his best friends would be drag queens, and every night would be a party; he would make it home well after midnight, sleep four or five hours, and be bright-eyed and bushy-tailed for work. Somehow, he managed it. In the four years between graduating from college and meeting Philip, he dated so many guys he lost track of their names. If he ran into them, at the supermarket or in a bar, there would always be an awkward few moments where Howard stood, squinting at the face that was just familiar enough, and searched his mind for the name to go with it. "Michael?" he would ask, because wasn't one in every five gay guys named Michael, anyway? Plus, he had dated three guys with the name, so it wasn't impossible.

"Jason," they'd say. Or Tom. Or Jeff. "You don't remember me?"

Apparently, it had been more memorable for them than it had for Howard. Or maybe they just had better memories than he did. Perhaps dating meant a lot more to them than it had to Howard, too. That wasn't to say that he always broke up with them; sometimes, he was the one who got dumped, graciously or unceremoniously. It was just dating. He was young and he was having fun—and a lot of sex. Because that was what young, attractive, upwardly mobile, gay men were supposed to do.

He was twenty-five when he met Philip. He was out with friends, waiting for the midnight drag show to start, and Philip just walked up and said hello. Howard had laughed, because in all the dating he had done in his short life, not a single guy had ever just walked up and introduced himself. There was always an intermediary—the guy's straight girlfriend, usually—who marched across the room to announce that her friend thought Howard was really cute, but he himself was too shy. That was one scenario, or he hooked up with the guy online, they had sex, and decided they might as well date and see how it goes.

"Are you laughing at me?" Philip had asked, and he clutched at his chest like it pained him, such an immediate rejection. He had smiled, though.

"No, no, no," Howard had answered, and he wanted it to be clear, because not only was Philip the first guy to ever just walk up and start talking to him, he was also the most attractive. "You're just the first guy who has ever taken it upon himself to break the ice." He offered his hand. "I'm Howard." Later, he would roll his eyes at the memory of offering Philip his hand to shake.

"Can I buy you a drink, Howard? My name's Philip."

They went to Philip's place, a smartly decorated loft in Midtown, for two reasons: Philip didn't have roommates, and Howard knew his bedroom was a mess, and he really wanted to make a good impression. They had sex and Howard spent the night, and in the morning it wasn't awkward when he awoke under strange sheets with his nose in Philip's armpit. When he tried to slip out of the bed without disturbing Philip, an arm swept him back, so he stayed the rest of the day. They listened to Nina Simone and Carole King and Shawn Colvin. They showered, then walked down the street for breakfast. They held hands and it still didn't feel awkward.

"You should just stay the rest of the day," Philip said, as if he were commenting on the weather.

"Yeah?" Howard regarded him over the rim of his latte mug, searching his face for some indication that he was just saying it because he felt obligated to.

Philip studied the table. "Yeah."

Weeks later, Howard would overhear Philip mention his boyfriend to someone and he would flinch, like he had been poked in the ribs. *Boyfriend.* There had been no formal conversation, wherein they sat and outlined the terms of their relationship and agreed on a title for one another: boyfriend, partner, whatever. Howard had stayed over that first night, then at Philip's request he'd stayed most of the rest of the day. They exchanged numbers when Philip loaded him into a cab for his ride back to the bar to collect his car. They saw one another three more times that week and kept an uninterrupted conversation going via text message. It was there they took care of the Q&A. Howard learned Philip was an interior designer; he confessed—and thank God it was through a text message—that he was a server. Philip did not miss a beat. *Wanna come over tonight?* he texted.

I work until midnight, Howard texted back.

Okay. See you then. ;)

Howard moved in first, and his clothes and possessions followed, one or two boxes at a time. Within six months, everything he owned had migrated from his apartment in the suburbs to Philip's loft.

"So... does this mean we're boyfriends?" he asked Philip that night in bed.

Philip had laughed. "If we were lesbians, it would mean we're married."

In fifteen years, they had come to know every inch of one another's bodies. Howard memorized every mole, every freckle, the curve of each lunula on Philip's fingernails, every crease in his knuckles. Caring for him since his release from the hospital, though, presented a sudden need for modesty on Philip's part. It bothered him, at first, when he couldn't bathe himself. "Embarrassing," he stammered. His cheeks were scarlet.

"I don't mind," Howard said, and he was surprised that he meant it. Intimacy had left nothing to the imagination.

"I do." But Philip just squeezed his eyes shut and turned away, like his not watching as Howard washed him would spare him the humiliation.

Judy helped with housework and errands when Howard would allow it, otherwise he did them late at night, when Philip was asleep. It was on one such occasion, as they argued over folding the clean laundry, that Judy asked what Howard himself had been wondering all along. "He's going to recover, right?"

"Of course he's going to recover," Howard snapped, then laughed so his mother wouldn't take it serious and dwell on the outburst for months, as was her nature.

"I mean *fully* recover," Judy said, undaunted. "You know... mentally...?"

Howard heaved a huge sigh and stared down at the t-shirt—one of Philip's—in his hands. He wondered the same thing daily, despite what the doctors and therapists at the rehabilitation center kept telling him. "He's going to make a complete recovery," they told him, and Howard would smile and thank them, then watch as Philip tried to relearn how to hold a pencil and sign his name.

"Yes," he told Judy, and gripped the t-shirt so tight his knuckles turned white. "It's just going to take a while."

It was Judy's turn to sigh. "I don't know how you do it, Howie." She hadn't called him that since he was in middle school. Hearing it nearly made him recoil.

"I do it because I love him, Mom," he said.

"Interesting," Judy said, more to herself than to him, and went back to sorting through the basket of laundry.

"What's that supposed to mean?" he asked, and didn't bother to laugh this time. He wanted his tone to be clear.

"Nothing," she said, and waved a hand, dismissing it. "Forget I said anything. I don't know what I'm saying."

"Bullshit," Howard said.

Judy acted shocked, but Howard didn't care. Anyway, he'd heard her say worse than that before, so he ignored her feigned astonishment and grabbed the hand she had waved so dismissively.

"Tell me what you meant," he said.

She sighed again. "It's just... I would never have done that for your father if he'd been unable to bathe himself or go to the bathroom alone," she said, color rising into her cheeks as her confession flowed forth. "And I loved your father. I did." She stared down at the basket of laundry as she spoke. "But he would have been ashamed. He would have been furious at me." She shook her head. "No. I would have hired a nurse or something. Why don't you do that?"

Howard released her hand and exhaled. "I'm not going to hire a nurse, Mom."

"I'm just saying."

"I know, but I can take care of him."

Howard cooked and he cleaned—and while he would never consider hiring a nurse, he seriously entertained the idea of hiring a maid. Philip progressed to using the bathroom by himself while Howard stood sentry on the other side of the door, straining his ears for even the slightest indication Philip might be having trouble. "You okay?" he called in.

"Fine," Philip shouted back. It took him a while that first time, but he eventually appeared in the door, leaning against the frame with sweat beaded on his forehead and what passed for an ear-to-ear grin since the accident. "Did it," he said.

Howard smiled, too, and blinked back the tears that threatened. He would truly be glad when they were on the other side of this and Philip was able to do all the things he had taken advantage of before. He was quite capable of caring for Philip, and would do whatever he needed to do, but it got tiresome. He wanted him well, whole again.

Philip got better with his words, too, and his speech slowly improved to the point where he was able to string more words together. The sutures were removed and he inspected his scar in the bathroom mirror. "I kind of... like it," he said, rubbing the lengthening black fuzz around it, turning his head to see it better. He grinned at Howard's appalled reflection in the mirror behind him, and Howard noticed for the first time that the top lid on his left eye drooped just a bit, giving him a lopsided look, like he might be sleepy.

"Your hair will grow in and cover it," he said.

Philip frowned. "I may keep... it short." He noticed his eye, blinked a couple times, took his finger and worked for a minute or two to make it look like the right eye, to no avail.

Howard inspected the network of scars peppering Philip's neck, his bicep, his ribs. They were livid red, but in time would fade and be practically invisible. "We can put cocoa butter on them," he said, more to himself than to Philip, thinking out loud. He ran his fingers down Philip's ribcage, so prominent now; he'd lost so much weight.

"They'll... fade," Philip said.

In another instant, Howard realized he'd become aroused; Philip noticed, too, and they moved together, it was awkward when they kissed. Howard snaked his hand into the shorts Philip was wearing, found him and stroked him. They stumbled, but Howard steadied them, leaned them both against the counter for support. He tried to remember the last time they had sex before the accident, but he couldn't, and then Philip was telling him to stop.

"It's no... use," he said, and laughed a little, but there was no mirth in it.

Howard pulled his hand away. "I'm sorry." He felt it important that he apologize.

"It's... me," Philip said without looking at Howard. "Not you." The back of his neck and ears glowed crimson as he pulled himself out of the bathroom and into the bedroom, his steps awkward and graceless as he made his way to the bed and settled onto the edge, panting.

Howard had no idea what to say, or if he should say anything at all. He stood there.

"Want to sleep," Philip told him, addressing the floor.

"Okay." Howard left him there on the edge of the bed. He went downstairs and cleaned the kitchen, took the trash out, ran a load of laundry. When he checked later, Philip was asleep, lying flat on his back as had become his habit since his extended stay in the hospital. It caused him to snore louder, another reason why Howard had decided to sleep in the guest room.

Later, they lay together watching TV. Philip had taken his medication, but was still alert as he waited for it to kick in. They chose a documentary on the prospect of colonizing Mars; comedies might make Philip laugh, and his ribs and midsection, though healed, couldn't take a lot of laughter, and there hadn't really been anything else of interest on, so they'd settled on the documentary in the hopes it would help Philip sleep.

"I'm sorry," Philip told Howard, without preamble, and for a second, Howard wasn't sure why. Then he remembered, just as Philip added, "About... sex."

Howard squeezed his hand under the blanket. "No. I shouldn't have tried to—"

Philip cut him off. "I guess the medicine... makes it hard." Then he considers what he just said and laughed. "Or... not."

Howard gave him a playful punch in the arm, but he laughed, too. "It's okay, though," he said. "Really."

But Philip shook his head. "No," he said, serious. His brow furrowed. He didn't look at Howard. "You... know you can—"

Howard cut him off then. "I know," he said, and he could hear the sharp tone in his voice, "but maybe I don't want to. Actually, I know I don't."

"Well... you can..."

"I know."

"...If you want to." Philip sighed and gave Howard's hand a gentle squeeze, then he was out like a light, his head lolling forward. Very gently, because he was afraid he would damage something and because Philip, though significantly thinner than before the accident, still outweighed him by a good fifty pounds, Howard settled him into a reclining position, pulled several of the pillows out from behind him, and turned the volume on the TV down. He slipped from the bed and studied Philip as he slept, like so many times since bringing him home from the hospital.

That first night had been the real ordeal, Howard jumping at every sound Philip made in his sleep, sure that every time he coughed, Philip would choke to death and he would be unable to save him. Now he contented himself with checking in every two hours or so, usually from the door, the bedside lamp illuminating Philip's supine position, the gentle rise and fall of his chest as he breathed. Still, though, there were nights when Howard strained his ears to hear snoring from across the hall and would come running to check that Philip hadn't stopped breathing, like a mother with a newborn infant must do.

When he was twelve, Howard learned that his mother had been having an affair with his pediatrician for most of his life.

It was Sunday and his father had insisted they spend the whole afternoon together. Judy had gone shopping, claiming a need for a new purse. Bob Koren would be flying out in the morning, to Seattle for a week-long convention. "We'll go see that movie you've been wanting to see," he said. "What's it called again?"

"*The Dark Crystal?*" Howard couldn't believe what he was hearing. "Really?" His father hated any and all movies that were not comedies or that were made after 1970.

"Yeah, really," Bob said, laughing. "You wanna see it, don't you?"

Howard made up his mind to move on it, before the offer was rescinded. He dressed and ran a comb through his hair, and was ready to go in five minutes.

"We can get dinner after," his father said. "Pizza?"

"Chinese!"

Bob slid *Black Gold* into the tape deck as he backed out of the driveway and the mournful voice of Nina Simone singing "Black Is The Color Of My True Love's Hair" filled the car. Howard made a face and turned away. The song creeped him out, something about the woman's voice. The way she sang it, he imagined the man she was singing about had died and she couldn't wait until she died, too, so they could be together again. His father never sang—"I couldn't carry a tune in a bucket!" Bob was often heard to say—but he whistled along as he drove.

Howard blocked the song by naming all the houses and businesses as they passed. *The Greenbergs live there... The Millers... Dr. Katz... Goldberg & Son Deli.* Bob stopped at a red light and the song ended, only to be followed by the same song sung by a man. He wanted to ask his father how he could listen to such depressing songs. How could they possibly put him in a good mood? But he knew his parents felt the same way about the music he listened to, and he didn't want to sound like them, nagging, so he kept his questions to himself.

The light changed and Bob drove on, whistling just under his breath to this new version of the song. *That's Dr. Stein's office...,* Howard thought to himself, and when he saw his mother's car, and his mother standing beside it, and Dr. Stein kissing his mother, he almost cried out, but caught himself just in time. What was he going to say? *Hey, Dad! I just saw Mom kissing Dr. Stein!* Then what? That they should turn around?

For a solid five minutes, Howard sat stock still in his seat and stared at the dash, processing what he'd seen. Dr. Stein, his pediatrician since birth, and his mother kissing. *But Mom's shopping,* he told himself. *Dad said so. She needed a new purse.* His heart pounded like a bass drum in his chest, his scalp and spine tingled, like he'd just had a fright. Like his mother and Dr. Stein had just jumped out at him from behind a bush as he was going along, minding his business, heading to the movies with his dad to see *The Dark Crystal.*

Bob sat, oblivious, behind the wheel, whistling along with Nina Simone. It was clear to Howard he had seen nothing.

At the theater, Bob bought them popcorn and soft drinks the size of pitchers. In the dark as they waited for the movie to begin, he offered the popcorn to Howard, who just shook his head. "It's got extra butter. You *love* extra butter."

"I'm not really all that hungry," Howard said, and hoped it was enough of an explanation.

His father gave him a quizzical look, and for a second Howard was afraid his father would pursue it: was he feeling good? was something the matter? what was wrong? do we need to call your mother? That was always Bob Koren's last resort. If he couldn't determine the cause of Howard's malaise, he handed the situation off to Judy. This time, though, he just shrugged. "Suit yourself," he said.

Howard sat in the dark and stewed. The previews began, and he was ready to consider that maybe he hadn't seen what he thought he'd seen. It had definitely been Dr. Stein, but maybe it was some other woman kissing him. There were lots of women in their early forties with dark hair pulled back with a banana clip, who dressed like that and drove the exact same car. It was a popular model. So, by the time the actual movie started, he had convinced himself that it was some other woman he'd seen kissing his pediatrician. He'd get home and there his mother would be, slightly irritated because she'd had to go to the mall (because she hated going to the mall), but she'd have her new purse, and Howard would feel dumb for even entertaining the idea that Judy Koren was cheating on her husband with her son's pediatrician.

He got to enjoy the movie, and he loved it, like he knew he would. His dad said he'd enjoyed it, but Howard knew better. Still, it was a pleasant, unexpected surprise and he was in a good mood when they went to get Chinese takeout. When they got home, Judy was in the kitchen, her cheeks flushed like she'd just run a race, but she smiled when she saw the food they'd brought. "Hope you don't mind Chinese," Bob said.

Judy laughed. "Are you kidding? I don't have to cook, and you think I'd *mind?*"

Howard studied her closely, as if there might be signs that she had been kissed, like Dr. Stein might have left some mark. He saw nothing, just her rosy cheeks, and the way she was smiling at everything. "Where's your purse?" he asked her.

"What?" Judy asked. From the look on her face, you'd think he had spoken a language she didn't understand.

"Dad said you were going to buy a new purse," Howard said.

"Oh." Judy waved a hand. "They didn't have the one I wanted."

Six months later, after the school year ended but before Howard left for Camp Barney, his parents

161

told him they wanted to talk to him, and he seriously thought they were going to surprise him with a trip to Europe or something, instead of JCC summer camp. So, he followed them into the den and seated himself on the ottoman, facing them where they sat on opposite ends of the sofa, and listened as, speaking in tandem, they told him they would be divorcing.

Howard just blinked. He searched for something adequate to say, but his mind was a total blank, so he sat there and blinked.

"Do you want to say something?" Judy asked.

Howard shook his head.

"Do you have any questions you want to ask us?" Bob asked.

And before he had really even thought about what he wanted to ask, or the words he needed to use, Howard turned to his mother and asked, "Are you—" He paused, realizing he wasn't sure how to say it. "—With Dr. Stein?"

Judy reacted like she had been slapped. She gaped at Howard, turned to Bob, found no support, and turned back to Howard. "What in the world makes you ask that, Howie?" In less than a second, her shock vanished and she was motherly again.

"I saw you guys kissing outside his office when Dad and I went to see *The Dark Crystal.*" There was no vitriol in his voice; he said it simply, like he was telling her what time it was.

Bob and Judy exchanged a look, then turned back to Howard.

"It's okay if you are," he said, with a small shrug.

Judy could only nod.

"So, who am I going to be living with?"

The truth was, Howard had so many friends whose parents had divorced, or who were going through a divorce, that he knew it really wasn't the major setback that some people would have him believe. It was divorce; no one was being executed. Bob wasn't even moving that far, only to Decatur. Howard would be able to see him whenever he wanted.

He didn't ask them for the reasons, but they gave them to him anyway: people get older and they change, and when they're young, people think things will last forever, but as they grow older and change, they realize that's not always the case, and so they grow apart. Howard listened, because he wanted to be polite, and nodded in all the right places, but he really just had one question for them.

"Am I going to have to miss Camp Barney because of this?"

His parents laughed. "No," Judy assured him. "Absolutely not. It's paid."

"Good."

So when he got back from camp in late July, Bob had moved out, and every room in the house seemed slightly askew with every trace of him gone from it. Howard walked each room slowly, searching for some tiny remnant, but Judy had apparently wiped all evidence of Bob from the house, since she couldn't do the same with her life. "Are you good, Howie?" she asked him, as he noticed all the missing books on the shelves in the den: all of Bob's John Updike and Pablo Neruda. Nothing was in their places and the empty slots on each shelf gave Howard the impression of mouths with missing teeth.

"Yeah," he told her. "I'm fine." And he was.

They spoke to Philip's doctor and were relieved to find out that brain injuries sometimes affected a man's ability to become aroused. It was the doctor's opinion that the condition was temporary, and they should see improvement as Philip's recovery progressed and the brain healed. "Sorry," Philip said on the drive home. He slumped in his seat, exhausted from the physical therapy and the sluggish pace of the recovery process in general.

"You don't have anything to be sorry for," Howard told him. "It's not like you did this to yourself."

Philip gave a small, barely audible grunt. He was silent for the rest of the drive, and when they got home he said he was tired and went to bed. Howard started a load of laundry and checked in to find Philip sound asleep, finally able to roll onto his side. It wasn't much, but it was progress. He scribbled a note and left it on the bedside table next to Philip's medication and water—*Gone to the store. Won't be long. Love you.* And a smiley face.

His list was small, so he planned to run in, grab what he needed, and run back out. He would be back home within thirty minutes; Philip would probably still be asleep and have no idea he'd even left. At any rate, that was his plan. He was rummaging through the potatoes, trying to find two potatoes that were the same size, when he heard his name.

"Howard?"

He turned and saw someone he didn't recognize.

"It is Howard, right?"

He nodded. "Yeah."

The guy stepped forward. "We used to work together," he said, and pointed to himself. "Jay. You probably don't remember me... it's been a while..."

Howard remembered him only vaguely, less because they had worked together and more because they'd had sex once. "No, no," he said, and smiled. "I remember you. How have you been? It *has* been a while." In his mind, he tried to remember just how long, but could only place it at six or seven years. He was actually surprised that this guy could remember him at all.

"I've been good," Jay said. "Working in Roswell now. You look great. Still working out..." Jay had hardly changed at all: different haircut, a beard now, he had neither lost weight nor gained; he was still chubby and pale to the point of being pink.

The truth was, Howard hadn't worked out since Philip's accident and he was starting to get soft. He'd noticed it in the shower one morning. Without thinking about it, he maneuvered his basket to hide his midsection. "Thanks," he said to Jay. "I've been a little slack lately, though."

Jay looked him over and shook his head. "It doesn't show," he said, and it was clear to Howard that he was being cruised. In the produce section of Whole Foods, of all places. He remembered the sex they'd had—drunken, clumsy, unsatisfying—but he felt himself aroused by the memory of it just the same.

Howard chuckled. "I wear it well, I guess." Then came that awkward silence that always arose when two people who had nothing else to talk about but sex ran out of things to say to pretend they weren't thinking of the sex they'd had. Howard held up the potatoes in his hands. "Well... I guess I should get to it," he said.

"Yeah," Jay said, crestfallen. "It was good seeing you again." Then his face lit up. "Hey, do you still have my number?"

Honestly, Howard had no idea. He'd been through so many cell phones since then. "I think so..."

"Let me give it to you." Jay did not ask it. He took out his phone and typed out a text message with his thumbs. "Let me know if you get it. Your number might have changed."

Howard blinked his surprise. *He still has my fucking number,* he thought just as his phone buzzed in his pocket. "I got it." He had to laugh.

"So, call me sometime," Jay said, and Howard expected him to actually lean in, wink, and lick his lips provocatively. He didn't, though.

He nodded. "I will," he said, and hurried away as fast as he could without seeming desperate to escape. He got everything he needed and checked out, already in a minor panic. What if Philip had woken up and found him gone? What if he was in pain? What if something else had happened? And he imagined all the worse possible scenarios as he checked out and raced to his car.

He was on his way out of the parking lot, calculating the time it would take to make it back home if he missed all the traffic lights—and if he got caught by them all—when he saw Jay walking to his car. He stopped alongside and rolled his window down, a nervous knot rising from his stomach to his throat, threatening to choke him. Jay stopped walking and grinned. "Well, that was quick," he said.

"What are you doing right now?" Howard asked. He had abandoned estimating the time it would take him to get home and was instead counting back to the last time he'd gotten a blow job.

Jay's apartment was tiny and cluttered and there was cat hair everywhere, but Howard resolved to ignore all that as he waited in the center of the cramped living room, ignoring the mess surrounding him, while Jay put his groceries away. "You want something to drink?" Jay called out to him.

"I'm good," Howard replied. *I just want my dick sucked.*

"Beer?"

"I'm good, really." *Can we just fucking do this, before I chicken out?*

Jay appeared, rubbing his hands on the front of his shorts in what might have been a gesture of nervousness had there not been such clear lust in his eyes as he leaned in and kissed Howard full on the mouth. It didn't surprise Howard, he'd seen it coming, but the force of it made him take a step back, and there was some quality to Jay's breath—not bad, exactly, just something—that he found unpleasant. Jay grabbed for him and pulled him close, snaked his arms under his t-shirt and found his nipples.

Howard turned his face out of the kiss.

"Let's go in the bedroom," Jay whispered, close to his ear, and Howard let himself be led there.

It was as untidy as the rest of the place, and Howard closed his eyes against it as Jay pulled his shirt over his head and moved to get him out of his shorts and shoes. It occurred to him that he should participate, so he rolled Jay's t-shirt up and over his head as Jay moved to kiss him again. He turned away

168

and Jay's mouth went to his neck, wet but not entirely unpleasant.

When they were naked, he almost laughed to find himself both repulsed and curiously turned on by the sight of Jay's belly and his fat, pink nipples. Jay lay against him and Howard marveled at the feel of him. He was firm where Howard had expected him to be soft and yielding, and he pressed himself hard against Howard's thigh.

"Tell me what you want," Jay sighed, close to his mouth, and again Howard had to turn away. He would have had a hard time explaining why if Jay had asked.

"Just give me head," he said, and threw an arm over his eyes as he felt Jay's mouth move down and take him in. And it was pleasant. He enjoyed it for about half a minute before he realized he couldn't do it. He sat up and said as much, and Jay stared at him, incredulous.

"What do you mean?"

"I have to go," Howard said. He stood and started gathering his clothes.

"Okay...," Jay said, and looked away. He pulled the wrinkled sheet over himself, suddenly modest.

It was always awkward when one person was more into it than the other, and doubly so when the one who wasn't into it didn't even want to see it through. Howard got dressed, checked his pockets to make sure nothing had fallen out. He wished there was some way of letting Jay know—and understand—that he wasn't the problem, but any way Howard phrased it in his mind to speak it sounded like the worst cliché in the world, so in the end he just said, "I'm really sorry."

Jay nodded. "It's okay," he said, but Howard knew it was everything but.

And before he even knew it, Howard was telling him about Philip's accident and the coma, and the weeks and months of recovery, of physical therapy, of speech therapy; how Philip was only just now getting the hang of how to hold a pencil again, and sign his name legibly. "He's got all his letters and numbers," he said, hearing himself and knowing he should shut up, but unable to stop the flow of words from his mouth. "His memory's been good, though, for the most part. I mean—he always knew who I was. He forgets the names of places, though. Sometimes."

Jay listened, gaped.

Howard told him about before the accident, how they had agreed upon the open relationship, and it had actually turned out *not* to be a problem for their relationship; neither of them had ever lost any interest in the other, and isn't that what an open relationship was supposed to be like?

"I guess...," Jay said.

Howard had his keys in his hand, and he spoke to them when he said, "Anyway, I was fucking some guy I don't even know when Philip had the accident." He paused, considered that last remark. It sounded like Philip had somehow been in control of the situation. It sounded wrong. "When he almost died," Howard added, and that felt better to say. "So, I'm sorry. Like I said. It's not you."

Then he left Jay sitting there, blinking, naked under a sheet, on the corner of his bed.

Philip was still sleeping when he got home, and Howard felt immense relief. He kicked his shoes off and got into the bed, on top of the blanket. Philip stirred, smiled, and as much as he could, pulled Howard to him. "There you are," he said.

"I went to the store," Howard said. "Did you wake up?"

"No," Philip said.

"Okay, good." He kissed the top of Philip's head, rubbed his chin against the unruly stubble. Very soon it would be long enough to curl, and it would be thick again, and as black as coal, the way Howard liked it.

A Map of the World

The first two times Rhonda got married, I wasn't able to be there. The first time—the summer after we graduated high school—I was in Europe, convinced it was the first step I needed to take to become the type of worldly, cosmopolitan person I'd always aspired to. I felt bad, in a way, because she'd asked me to be her best man (and we'd laughed about the effect *that* would have on our small East Tennessee town), but not too bad because I was having a lot of really good sex with a lot of really hot guys across Europe. They divorced after a year and a half, so I didn't regret it for long. The second time, she eloped and called me from Las Vegas at three in the morning. His name was Rod, if I remember correctly, and I found that supremely funny at the time.

This time, she assures me over the phone, is the last. "But you have to be my best man this time, and don't tell me you have something else planned."

"Well, when is it?"

"The twelfth of June," she tells me.

As it turns out, I have nothing planned until the weekend of Labor Day, but when she tells me the date, I dread it immediately. Tennessee in June is only slightly cooler than the surface of the sun. "Is it outside?" I ask.

"God, no!"

"Okay, then, yes."

She squeals, and I laugh, then she tells me her colors—teal and magenta—and I have to actually think if teal is still a preferred wedding color, when she asks me if I have heard about Rowdy.

"What about him?" I ask, trying to sound indifferent, even as a chill is creeping up my spine. There is no way any news of Rowdy, after all this time, can be good news.

"Well... somebody killed him," she says. She whispers it, like she might be next if someone heard her. "They found him up on Windrock with his throat cut."

A minute ago, I was breaking a sweat thinking of Rhonda's wedding in June. Now I'm cold as ice and I can't even think of what's appropriate to say. I haven't spoken to Rowdy since my senior year of high school; I haven't even thought of him that often. Now Rhonda is telling me he's dead and I feel guilty for something I'm not quite certain of.

"You there, Danny?" she asks me.

"Yeah," I say.

"I figured your mom would have told you," Rhonda says. "They're saying it was drugs."

I think *Drugs slit his throat?* Then I realize what she means is Rowdy's murder is drug-related and that makes more sense. "Do they know who did it?" I ask.

173

"Not yet."

"That sucks," I say, then try to switch my mood back to better match the news of her wedding. "Anyway, I'm putting it on the calendar and I'll definitely be there."

"You'll have to help me plan!" she says, and I'm not sure how I'll do that from Dallas, but she is undaunted. "I'll email you all my ideas and you can help me pick what'll work. You know I was never good at stuff like that. Not like you."

People always say they met in kindergarten, and I've always thought that's embroidering it a bit. Children don't operate that way. Rhonda and I were in the same kindergarten class and when it was time to play, we started playing together. I don't even think I knew her name for three weeks; she was just a girl with pigtails, and she liked doing the same things I liked doing—the monkey bars, especially—so we bonded. There was no formal greeting, no exchange of names. We were both there and we started playing together on the monkey bars.

Rowdy came along in fourth grade. He was easy to overlook, and he was the new kid, and he had a funny name, so the ones who didn't pick on him just avoided him. Rhonda would have ignored him completely, but I felt sorry for him when I saw him alone on the playground and suggested we let him play on the monkey bars with us.

"Just leave him alone," she said. "He's weird."

I wasn't convinced. "We should be nice to him," I told her. "He's new here. He doesn't have any friends."

"Whatever."

He was small, even for a nine-year-old, and thin. "Hey," I said, by way of introduction. "You want to play with us?" I nodded back over my shoulder to where Rhonda was executing a death-defying handstand on the top of the monkey bars.

"I'm new here," he said, as if his status might make him ineligible to play. His voice was small, like him.

"I know," I said, and laughed because it was funny that he'd pointed out something everyone already knew. "My name's Danny. And that's Rhonda." We both watched her walk on her hands to the edge of the bar she was on and do a near perfect dismount, like a gymnast in jeans and a *Mork & Mindy* t-shirt.

"I can't do stuff like that," he said, his eyes wide.

"I can't either. Rhonda's just showing off. Come on."

So he joined us on the monkey bars, and he sat with us in the cafeteria, and Rhonda, even if she did consider him weird for whatever reason, became his de facto protector against the bigger boys who would try to bully him or the girls who would make fun of him because he was small, or because his name was Rowdy.

"That's like a name you give your dog," Rhonda commented once, and that made Rowdy smile. She wasn't being mean, she was just stating a fact.

"Yeah," was all he said, though.

As it turned out, Rowdy lived down the road from me, so we would walk home together after school. Rhonda took the bus.

He was quiet, kicking rocks as we walked along on the precarious shoulder of the road. I asked him the usual questions: what TV shows did he like? did he like comic books? did he like Foreigner? had he seen *Star Wars?* He liked *Superfriends* and *Three's Company*, he told me; he hadn't seen *Star Wars*, and I was incredulous, but he explained that he didn't get to see many movies because his dad was a long haul trucker and his mom worked third shift at the hosiery mill. He said Foreigner was okay, but he liked Kiss better, and he didn't get to read too many comics.

"I'll let you read some of mine," I told him. "I have lots."

"Okay," he said, neither enthused nor uninterested.

We were in the eighth grade before I learned Rowdy lived in the middle of the junk yard at the end of my road. I imagined it to be the coolest place in the world to live; Rhonda was dubious. "He lives in a *junkyard,"* she said, and made a face, as if the notion of it might sicken her.

"I know. Isn't that cool?" I lived with my mother and my older sister, and we lived next door to my grandmother. This was standard practice in Appalachia, but in my mother's defense, she had moved away to get married, then moved back, into the house where she had grown up. My grandmother, widowed, moved next door over my mother's protests. I thought Rowdy's situation was exponentially superior to my own. A junkyard and not overrun with women? I wanted to go there, spend as much time as I could there, but there was always an excuse why we couldn't hang out at his house, so we hung out at mine.

"He eats like he's starved half to death," Mama said to me one night after Rowdy had gone home and she was clearing away the dishes.

"So does Danny," my sister pointed out.

"Not like that. Not like Rowdy." I knew what she meant: Rowdy wolfed down food like he never got any unless he got it at our house. And it occurred to me that could be the reason he never wanted me to come to his place, though I desperately wanted to see what life inside a junkyard was like. I imagined it to be magical, with tunnels and hiding places built into and through the mountains of refuse, with rats the size of dogs who were intelligent, domesticated creatures and would eat out of your hand, the way rodents in movies did. I imagined Rowdy having his choice of places to sleep every night—an abandoned camper, the back seat of a long-forgotten Edsel, or a centuries-old iron bed out in the open—as fireflies danced above it all, like fairies.

"It's just a trailer," he said, when I urged him to at least tell me what it was like. "And it's not in the middle of the junkyard, it's at the back of it, against the fence. We rent it from the guy that owns it. He had a house built."

I was undeterred. "It still has to be better than living in a house full of women," I said.

Rowdy laughed. "I guess. I'm alone most of the time."

I wanted to go to the junkyard and, if nothing else, just dig through it. I was convinced I would find something of enormous value there, like a box of rare, first issue comics in the trunk of a rusty Cadillac, or the props from some horror film from the Fifties. The chances were slim, but I held out hope.

"It's not really like that," Rowdy explained as we pushed our bikes home from school one day. "It's mostly cars and car parts. Stuff he can sell and make money on."

He evoked pity from some—my mother, my grandmother, me—and apathy from most, like Rhonda and the kids at school who'd long grown tired of bullying him or making fun of his name, since it never elicited any real response from him. Now they just left him alone. Rhonda's ability to completely disregard Rowdy, even when they sat across from one another during lunch, was impressive. At that age, I didn't have the words for it, but there was something tragic about Rowdy, and I felt it even if I couldn't explain it. I felt obligated to protect him from the stinging barbs of the other kids, and if I couldn't do that, at least make him feel better in the wake of them. He was always smaller than the other boys, even me, but once we reached high school, he started to fill out. He left middle school a runt and reported to high school more of a bantam.

Rhonda regarded him with disdain, but other girls—those who'd attended other middle and elementary schools—were beginning to notice him. I was irritated by it, the way they tittered amongst themselves like birds as they walked by us in the halls, looking back over their shoulders to see if he'd noticed them the way they'd noticed him. Rowdy was completely oblivious, and that pleased me, which confused me at first. We were a month into our freshman year when I realized I, like all those silly girls, was attracted to Rowdy.

Mama was legitimately upset when I told her I wouldn't be staying with her while I was back for Rhonda's wedding. By this time, Mammaw had moved back in with her and they rented the house next door. "A real nice Mexican family," she said, as if it surprised her that Mexicans could be nice. "He works down at the Food City and she cleans houses." Then she remembered that she was supposed to be mad at me. "But why don't you stay here?"

"I already got the room," I said.

Mammaw smoked her cigarette and grunted. "Well, you got more money than you got sense, I reckon," she said, and I noticed she didn't have her teeth in.

"It's the Holiday Inn in Harriman," I told them. "It's not The Ritz."

Mama lit a cigarette and they both smoked, which is a large part of why I didn't want to stay with them. I'd only recently quit and knew their chain smoking would be more temptation than I could handle, especially once Rhonda and I started drinking. "Well, it hurts my feelings you don't want to stay here," she said, and I knew she wasn't serious. Something in her tone.

I rolled my eyes. "No it doesn't, Mama."

She ignored that. "And I got your room ready for you, too."

I went to see it, even though I wouldn't be staying there. Mama had changed nothing about the room since I'd vacated it after high school, other than to move her sewing machine into a corner near the window. The bed was the same, the bottom half of a set of bunk beds that had been separated, the other one lost and forgotten. On the wall above it hung an outdated map of the world, its edges ragged, curling and starting to yellow. I'd stripped the walls of everything else before I moved out—posters of celebrities and rock stars, mostly, with Einstein and Shakespeare thrown in to give a sense of ambition. I'd left the map, all the push pins—mine red, Rowdy's blue—intact because I had intended to check my progress whenever I returned home.

I went to it now, peered close at the places where we'd stuck our pins. San Francisco, Puerto Rico, Miami; I carefully removed the pins I'd placed over those cities I'd visited. Tokyo stayed, and Sydney, and Auckland. I wondered if I'd ever make it to any of those places now.

Most of the pins were mine, maybe twenty were Rowdy's. His wanderlust had been more practical than mine. He'd pinned Dallas, Houston, Albuquerque, Los Angeles, then—half a world away— a blue pin protruded from Moscow, part of the Soviet Union then. I smiled as I recalled Rowdy putting it there, even as tears blurred my vision.

He was never really good at school. Some people just aren't, and I know that now, but back then I thought I could help him, make him better at it by showing him how I did it. And he tried. He listened to everything I said and attempted to recreate it on paper—diagramming sentences, finding the common denominator—but always to no real avail. He passed, but barely, and it never seemed to matter to him, anyway.

"You need to know this stuff, Rowdy," I told him.

"No, I don't," he replied.

"What about college?"

That made him laugh. "I'm not going to college, Danny."

I knew that, of course, but I wanted to think that Rowdy would get out of Roane County like I planned to. "Well, even if you end up running a register at Food City, you need to know math," I countered, intent on winning this argument.

He laughed and pushed his books away, reclined back onto my pillows. We always studied at my house, never at his, and I had stopped trying to wrangle an invite. His parents had since divorced, his mother moving out west with someone she'd worked with at the hosiery mill. Rowdy's father was still gone most of the time, but when he was home I noticed the change in Rowdy and saw the marks on his neck, under the collar of his shirt, and on his arms, barely visible under the sleeve of his shirt. I wanted to ask, but I knew it would infuriate and embarrass Rowdy, and anyway, it was clear what happened: Rowdy and his father fought, probably because his dad drank, either as the cause or the result of his mother running off with another man.

I stretched out beside him, pretending to stare hard at the equation we had been tackling. Rowdy stretched like a cat, and put his arms behind his head. I breathed in the smell of him, a bouquet that was pure Rowdy: deodorant that had stopped working hours ago and his own musk, something like fallen leaves and honey.

This was how it had begun, with me pretending I was studying and Rowdy pretending he was stretching, but that first time he'd started rubbing himself through his jeans, I thought I would choke on my own lust for him, and when he said "Why don't you do it instead...," I barely heard him over the pounding of my blood in my ears. The whole situation was so unbelievable, I felt myself about to laugh, but I didn't want to miss the opportunity, so I took him up on the offer before it was rescinded.

The first few times, I just jacked him off. We advanced to me sucking him off after about a month, and by sophomore year, he was fucking me. We didn't kiss, though. I tried once, desperate for it, and he turned away with a simple, "No. Not that." I was disappointed, but I took what I could get. And at first I was terrified we'd be caught by my mother or my grandmother, less from shame than the prospect that they would prohibit Rowdy from coming over and forbid us from seeing one another altogether. So we locked the door and played music, but there was still noise.

"You okay?" Rowdy would ask me afterwards, and my emotions would swell.

"Yeah," I said.

"You're sure?"

"Yeah."

Later—after we'd been regularly fucking for six months—I learned it wasn't tenderness that made him ask it, but a genuine concern: he didn't want to cause any damage and me end up in the emergency room explaining how it had happened, then him getting into trouble. I couldn't imagine what kind of trouble he thought would come from it, but Rowdy lived in fear of a vague *trouble* he could never really define or clarify. It would have to do for tenderness.

I was surprised no one ever suspected anything. At least no one let on that they did. Rowdy and I would come in through the kitchen after school. "You staying for dinner, Rowdy?" Mama would ask him as she peeled potatoes.

He always acted as if he weren't sure, as if he would have to check and get back with her on it.

"We have plenty," she said, and never looked up.

"Thank you, ma'am." For someone so rough and uncultured, the manners Rowdy displayed toward his elders—women especially—always caught me off guard. His fingernails were ragged, bitten and blackened by motor oil, his clothes wrinkled and often musty-smelling, but he was as mannerly as a suitor when he needed to be. It melted my heart. He was, of course, oblivious.

In stark contrast to those genteel manners was his temper, which could come out of nowhere at any moment, and which kept him in trouble throughout middle school and into high school. Fights sent him to the principal's office at least once a week, and twice got him in-school suspension. High school was somewhat easier for him. By then, most people knew Rowdy and were aware of his reputation and thus chose not to provoke him. Still, though, there were those, mostly boys like Rowdy, from unstable homes missing one parent or the other, who seemed intent on provoking him, or he them. They took these fights off school grounds, at least.

"You're lucky someone didn't call the cops," I told him after one of those fights. We were in the bathroom at my house and I was cleaning him up. Rowdy sat on the edge of the tub while I knelt in front of him with a bottle of alcohol.

"That guy started it," he grumbled through a split, swollen lip.

"So, they'd take you both to jail." I soaked a cotton ball with alcohol. "This is gonna sting."

He flinched. "I ain't worried about that," he said, and I had no doubt he wasn't. It worried me, though, and I wondered what his reaction would be if I told him so. I imagined him flinching, like when I touched the alcohol to the gash in his lip.

"Well, you should be," I said, and realized I sounded like Mama.

"He started it, though," Rowdy said again. "What was I s'posed to do, just let him kick my ass?"

I heaved a sigh. "Hold this on your lip until the bleeding stops." I pressed a wad of toilet tissue against the cut and turned my attention to his knuckles. He sucked in his breath and winced when I poured alcohol over them, but otherwise held his tongue.

Later, he dozed on my bed while I perused catalogs from prospective colleges. I will be a junior next year, and I have decided I want to narrow the field. The only thing I know for certain is that I want to go somewhere out of state—California, Washington, Maine. The very idea thrilled me and terrified me at the same time.

"What are these?" he asked, drowsy, holding one up that had poked him in the ribs.

"Colleges I'm considering."

He gave me a derisive grunt and rolled over to face the wall.

"You know, you need to start considering what you're gonna do after school, too," I said.

"I'll get a job somewhere and work," he replied.

It sounded bleak to me, and as on many occasions with Rowdy, my heart broke. Of course college wasn't an option for him. "You should do something with cars," I suggest. "You're good with cars."

His reply was a grunt, neither for nor against the idea.

"Or you could do something with your art." Rowdy was actually very good at drawing comic book-style characters and scenes. I guess he honed his skill by doodling in class when he should have been listening.

That made him laugh. "Like what? Go to art school? Yeah, right..." He rolled onto his back and stretched. I heard every part of him crack—toes, back, neck, fingers. "College is for people like you, Danny. People like me get a job at the mill or Food City."

I knew he was telling the truth. We were surrounded by people who had done just that—

graduated high school, got a job, and stayed. My mother had actually left; she'd refused to be a part of that statistic, so she'd left town the day after she graduated high school and gone as far away as she could on what little money she'd had at the time, which turned out to be Panama City, Florida. She was lucky and got a job waiting tables on the beach, where she met my father and got pregnant with my sister all within her first three months there. They never married, because to hear her tell it, once tourist season ended, they both got too busy trying to find and keep work that getting married just didn't seem that important. But he drank, and when he drank he got mean, so she packed up and, pregnant with me, returned home one night. She'd been away just over two years.

The next week, I stole a fold-out map of the world from the library at school when it fell out of the *National Geographic* I was reading for a report on damage to the ozone layer. I hung it on the wall above my bed and stuck pins into each of the cities where I might go to college. Then I spread out from there to include places I would like to travel—Rome, Vienna, Helsinki—or live, like Honolulu or San Francisco or Los Angeles.

"What are the pins for?" Rowdy asked. I had just given him a blow job and he was stuffing himself back into his underwear when he noticed the map.

"Places I want to go," I said.

187

He got on his knees on the bed and peered at the map, the cities I had chosen. "Why these places?" he asked, without a trace of scorn or sarcasm.

I shrugged. "I dunno. They're just away from here, and they sound interesting."

He grunted. "Why this place in particular?" He pointed to Helsinki. He didn't say the word; he didn't want to mispronounce it.

I shrugged. "It sounds about as far away from here as you can get," I said. "Reykjavik, too."

"Where's that?" he asked, searching the southern hemisphere and up the Pacific Rim.

I pointed it out to him.

"Iceland." He whispered it. "I'll bet it gets cold there."

"Actually, Helsinki is colder."

Rowdy grunted, but whether or not he believed me wasn't clear.

I told him then of how, when I was in the fourth grade, I went through the glossary at the back of my social studies book and wrote out the name and definition of every foreign city and country listed there. When he asked why, I couldn't say exactly; if it had been assigned, I'm sure I would have resented such a tedious task. "I think because I just wanted to be sure that there were other places in the world," I said. By then we were lying on our backs, head to foot, like sardines in a can. I gazed up at the map.

"My father was from Cuba." I located it on the map and pictured palm trees and houses painted the blue of the ocean and the yellow of butter.

Rowdy sat up and scowled at me. "Then why don't you have a Cuban last name?"

"They were never married, so we got Mama's last name," I explained.

It seemed to satisfy him. "Oh," he said.

I gestured at the map with my chin. "Where would you go, Rowdy? If you could go anywhere in the world?"

He sat up and stared hard at the map, like it might reveal to him where he should want to go. Like the name of the city might glow with his longing to go there. "I don't know," he said. "I never really thought much about it."

"Well, now's your chance." I sat up and grabbed my box of push pins. He picked a few blue ones out and got to his knees before the map, studied it, like he was being tested and didn't want to give the wrong answer. "Anywhere you want to go."

He took forever and it occurred to me as he agonized over his choices—a literal world of them— that he was having such difficulty because it had never crossed his mind that he could, if he chose, go anywhere in the world. Not like me. I seemed to have started my wanderlust young, and would see to it that I did not get trapped in Roane County for the rest of my life, or (and sometimes, I think this was worst) get out the way mama did, only to return, defeated, because I had no other options. I might not make it as far as Reykjavik or Helsinki, but I would make it somewhere.

Rowdy stabbed a pin into Miami. "Disneyworld's in Miami, ain't it?"

"Orlando."

He moved the pin. I swallowed the lump in my throat. Of all the places he could have chosen, Rowdy wanted to go to Disneyworld.

Rhonda wanted to drink and told me so when she called me. "You checked in?" she asked, breathless, as if she were the one who'd just dragged everything from the car to the room. "Let's go drink!" I thought to point out to her that she had a bachelorette party scheduled for later, but knew it was pointless.

I waited for her in the hotel lounge. She came in like a dervish, screaming and reeking of cigarettes and some perfume no one else wore anymore. She had changed and she was exactly the same. Physically, there was still the mane of hair—a honey blonde now—and the bold prints, but she had put on a lot of weight and was wearing entirely too much makeup during the day for a woman her age. But she acted the same as she had her entire life: loud, bossy, unashamed.

"Oh my god, look at you!" She held both my hands in hers and inspected me the way a grandmother would a child—head to toe and back again. She even spun me around.

"What?" I asked, never used to such scrutiny.

"You look *amazing!* Do you *ever* age?" She laughed. I thought I looked my age; looking younger had never been a real priority of mine.

"You look good, too, Rhonda." I was trying to remember the last time I'd seen her. Four years ago? Or five? She'd come to Dallas with some girlfriends and had insisted that I join them for a girl's night out. I'd ended up being a chaperone, basically, for a group of women who drank like they were in college, but were old enough to know better. I listened to them complain about their husbands or boyfriends, or about being single if they had neither, and pretended not to see them flirt and throw themselves at bartenders and bouncers and random men in every bar and restaurant we went to. I was glad she'd come alone, but I suspected the gaggle of girlfriends would be a significant part of the bachelorette party tonight.

She dismissed my compliment with a wave of her hand. "You don't mean that, Danny, but it's nice of you to say so."

"No, really," I insisted.

"Whatever. Let's have a drink." She sat at the bar and waved to the bartender. "I'll have a Cadillac margarita!" He looked at me, but I held up my beer, which I'd barely touched and was getting warm. "Danny'll have one, too!" I started to protest, but she silenced me with a hand. "Tell it to the hand, boyfriend!"

191

I cringed, but managed to smile. The bartender left us.

"I bet you can't smoke in here," Rhonda said, and searched for an ashtray. "You just about can't smoke anywhere these days."

"Well, maybe that's a good thing," I suggested.

She threw me a look. "Whatever. You used to smoke like a freight train yourself, mister, so don't act all high and mighty about smoking."

"I was just saying..."

The drinks came and she forgot about smoking. "He's cute, don't you think? The bartender?"

I laughed. "Did you forget you're getting married tomorrow?"

She rolled her eyes. "Not for me, dumbass! For *you!*"

It was my turn to roll my eyes. "Yeah, right." I sipped the margarita and was immediately reminded why I never drink them. "So, who's this guy you're marrying?" I would talk about anything to steer her away from any discussion about my love life and lack of a boyfriend. "Did he go to school with us?" I tried to recall his name from the invitation, but couldn't. I could remember clearly that Rhonda's middle name was Lurlene, which had surprised me for some reason. How had I never known that?

"Oh, no, he's older," she said. I wondered if my sister would know him.

She told me about meeting him—in Panama City, wasn't that funny?—and not really being attracted to him at first, but wasn't that always the case? His name was Eddie, but it wasn't short for Edward, and he owned a bike shop. "Motorcycles," she said, to clarify. "Not bicycles."

"Cool," I said, but I wasn't impressed and hoped it didn't show.

"He has three kids, so I'll be a step mom, but they're older, so it's not like I'll be raising them, you know?" She drained her glass and held it up for a refill. It was going to be a long night if she was already drinking like this and we were still hours from her bachelorette party.

"So, where is this party again?" I asked her.

"My friend Misty's place. She has a pool."

Later, as I drove us there, Rhonda mentioned Rowdy. She was not as drunk as she should have been after consuming three of the Cadillac margaritas at the hotel. "I know I was never all that nice to him when we were growing up," she said, and sounded genuinely remorseful, "but we were kids, you know? And kids can be real assholes sometimes." She chuckled. "Hell, I have four, so I should know."

"We were all assholes back then," I said. It sounded better than correcting her and saying she hadn't been an asshole so much as she'd been a real bitch, and especially to Rowdy.

"Not you, though," she said. "You were always sweet."

I rolled my eyes. "I was *not* always sweet."

"Whatever," Rhonda said. "You were a good kid, and you were smart, and you didn't give your mama anything to worry about. Not like I did. God, I was a hellion, wasn't I?" She laughed and gave me a punch on the leg. "It's a wonder I made it out of high school alive."

In high school, she had been one of those girls with a reputation—two of them, actually: one as the toughest girl in school and the other as the easiest lay. Rhonda had worn both labels proudly. I still blink in surprise to know that I, essentially a nerd, had been her friend at all, but such were the bonds of friendship forged so early in life.

"You know, Rowdy was a good kid, too," she said, softer, staring out the window into the dusk. "It's awful what happened to him."

I am quickly choked by a hot knot of sadness and horror. "What *did* happen, actually?" She told me his throat had been slit and I just couldn't reconcile that with rural East Tennessee. A slit throat suggested hired assassins—the yakuza, ninjas, the Russian mafia—not crystal meth addicts in Appalachia. Then again, what the hell did I know about the lengths to which people would go for drugs. That addiction, luckily, had never been a problem for me. "Did they ever find who did it?"

Rhonda nodded. "A bunch of kids. Ain't that something?" She fished in her purse and brought out her cigarettes, then seemed to remember she was a passenger in my car and put them away again.

"You can smoke," I told her, though I knew it would take months to get rid of the smell.

"Thank God." She rolled the window down and lit one, picked up her account of Rowdy's murder. "Three kids, and the girl was still in high school, though I think they're gonna try her as an adult, considering what they did to him." She paused to exhale. "And she's the one that ended up telling everything. I reckon she thought it might get her some leniency with the judge, or some plea deal. You know, they can plea bargain just about anything these days, even if there are a hundred witnesses that see you do it, you can still make a deal." Another pause. "Anyway, she said they owed Rowdy money—well, her boyfriend did; he was the oldest of the three of them—and Rowdy called them up, threatening him she claims, so they agreed to meet Rowdy out somewhere and when he got there, she says, the boyfriend said Rowdy could ride with him to wherever—I think she said it was an uncle's place out in Coalfield—so Rowdy got in the car with them."

"Well that was stupid," I muttered, like I was an authority.

"The girl says they were all friends, actually, so maybe Rowdy didn't think anything of getting in the car." Rhonda shrugged. "Anyway, she says they drove out toward Coalfield like they were really going somewhere, but once they were out on Coal Hill Road, the boyfriend—he was in the back seat with Rowdy—took out a knife and did it. Slit his throat." She paused and there was a surprised look on her face, like she was hearing for the first time as she told it. "Just like that."

"Damn," I said, trying to picture what Rowdy might look like with his throat slit from ear to ear, gasping for breath through a severed windpipe. I could only conjure memories of him in his dingy white briefs, or naked, his uncircumcised penis looking a lot like an elephant's trunk.

"Oh! Here we are," Rhonda said. "This is Misty's place. Turn in here."

The guests for the bachelorette party were a motley crew, men and women of all ages. The men were all gay, of that I was certain the instant I am through the door. Misty could be Rhonda's twin. They're the same size and shape, they had the same hairstyle (Misty's was bleached blond), and their makeup was identical. They were even wearing the same maxi dress, Rhonda's pink and Misty's green.

"I thought you'd never get here, bitch!" she said and slapped a cheap, plastic tiara onto Rhonda's head. Everyone cackled like hens.

"This is Danny, everybody!" Rhonda grabbed me and spun me around to face everyone: Julie, Kayla, Carol Ann, Becky. There was no way I would be able to remember all these names. "And this is Misty's nephew, Justin."

I knew exactly what was happening, and I wasn't having it. I smiled politely to Justin, said hi. "Y'all should talk!" Misty declared.

"Is there a beer?" I asked Rhonda.

"You have to meet everyone first," she said, and spun me some more. Kaylee (not to be confused with Kayla), Amy, Leigh Anne. "And this is my uncle Melvin and his friend Randall." She did not have to tell me what *friend* meant, but she leaned in and whispered. "They're partners. You know, like boyfriends...? They live together, going on twenty years now."

"Rhonda's told us so much about you," said Melvin, and I saw that he was missing teeth. He took my hand and didn't shake it so much as he held it between his own. Randall smiled at me from behind Melvin and he, too, was missing teeth

"So nice to meet you both," I said, and in a whisper to Rhonda: "I need that beer."

She got it for me and I escaped with it out the back door, onto Misty's deck overlooking the pool. I feared there would be skinny dipping later, and knew I needed to escape long before that happened. Then I realized that this was really the first time I'd had alone with my thoughts since I got into town, and I immediately thought of Rowdy, his throat cut, his dead eyes frozen in surprise, his body tangled in briars on Windrock. And I wondered if he'd ever made it to Disneyworld.

The door behind me slid open and Justin crept out onto the deck. "Am I bothering you?" he asked in a whisper.

I shook my head. "I just needed some air."

He grinned and glanced back over his shoulder. Inside, country music was blaring and Rhonda and Misty were gyrating. "I can't imagine why," he said, and we laughed.

"Rhonda's always been a wild woman," I told him.

He leaned against the rail and lit a cigarette. I considered asking him if he was old enough, but caught myself. I'd smoked through high school and no one had ever given me that passive-aggressive guilt trip. "Y'all grew up together?"

"Since kindergarten."

His eyes widened, and I could tell he was thinking something along the lines of *Wow, I'm surprised they even had kindergarten back then!* But he says, "That's a long time."

I laugh. "Yeah, we're old."

He laughed, too, but I'd embarrassed him. "That's not what I meant at all. I just meant..." He had to stop to collect his thoughts, put them into words. "That's a long time to know someone and still be friends."

"Yeah," I said, and glanced in at the party. I couldn't see exactly what Rhonda and Misty were doing, but everyone else was cheering them on.

"Rhonda says you live in Dallas," Justin said.

I nodded. "Yeah."

"And you're an artist?"

"*Graphic* artist," I said, but that was a lie. I'd been one, had gone to school for it, but I'd been impatient in my twenties, and when I didn't get rich enough fast enough, I'd given it up to wait tables until I could find something better. That was what I told myself at the time, because surely the offers would come pouring in just as soon as I put myself out there as available. That was twenty years ago, and I'd been working in a bank for the past seven. Of course, I didn't mention that.

"I'm looking at art school," he said. "Savannah College of Art and Design?"

Maybe this was why Rhonda thought we should talk, and not because we were both gay like I'd thought before. "It's not easy," I told him. I'd done the same thing, basically: graduated high school and moved down that summer to start school. It was like moving to another country and I hadn't been ready for it. I partied too much and struggled with my classes when I should have breezed through, like high school. But Roane County didn't have gay bars and drag shows and male strippers, and Dallas had all that and more. I let it consume me and I suffered for it. I graduated, but with a GPA I would have been ashamed of in high school, and that meant I didn't get on at the better companies for the better pay; I had to settle for what I could get, and I was too young to commit to reinventing myself as a working graphic artist, instead of an art student, so when the money didn't come, I took the easy way out and became like everyone else I knew at the time—we all had degrees, but we waited tables and tried to convince everyone (and ourselves) that we chose to do so.

"Is anything easy, though?" he asked with a grin, and I wished I'd had the same philosophy when I was his age.

"I guess not." We both turned at the sound of knocking to see Rhonda gesturing for us to come inside. "I guess we should join the party, huh?"

Misty had planned a series of games, all involving the consumption of alcohol and with the sole purpose of embarrassing Rhonda as much as possible. I participated half-heartedly until the stripper arrived, then saw my chance to escape. Rhonda was pretending to hide her eyes, but I saw her peeking between her fingers.

"You leaving, sweetie?" Melvin asked me as I passed the kitchen on my way to the front door.

"I'm exhausted," I said, which was true. "I didn't get a nap in after the drive up, so I'm calling it a night."

"See you at the wedding, though?"

"Of course."

The wedding was at two in the afternoon, so I slept in the next morning. Because there was something luxurious about sleeping late in a hotel room, those crisp sheets and oversized pillows. And when I couldn't sleep any longer, I just lay there and stared at the ceiling and wondered about Rowdy. Did he know, when he got into that car, that he was going to his death, or did he realize it somewhere along the way? And what would it be like to know you were going to die. Did he put up a fight? He'd always been so quick to fight through school. Or did it take him completely by surprise? He met up with them and they discussed the money they owed him, and surely he was pissed. Surely he stomped around and threatened whichever one of them it was who owed him, so they told him—lied to him—that they could get the money from someone (had Rhonda said the girl said it was an uncle?), so they'd got into the car to drive there.

Had he known? I doubted it. Rowdy wasn't the most intelligent person in the world, but he knew better than to get into a car with people who seemed a threat. So, it must have taken him by surprise. Maybe when they'd turned onto Coal Hill Road, he'd sensed something was wrong and asked where the hell it was they were taking him. But they'd already lied—there was no money—so they kept lying to him. The uncle lived in Coalfield, maybe; it didn't seem too far-fetched. But I doubt he anticipated the knife being drawn and slashing his throat. How the hell would anyone anticipate something like that? And he'd probably been selling to those kids for years. How was he to know they'd end up killing him?

It made me sad knowing that Rowdy was dead and knowing how he had died, and why. It made me sad because I hadn't bothered to keep in contact with him for the past twenty-seven years, and it made me even sadder that I thought if I had called him or written him that he wouldn't be dead now. Like I could have saved him from those kids, or from selling drugs in the first place.

When I left that summer after graduation, two weeks before my classes started, I'd gone to see him at the body shop where he was working. He'd dropped out of school the year before, despite my protests. Now he worked, painting cars and restoring dents and tinting windows at a place a mile further up the road from the junkyard. He was surprised to see me. "You needing some work done?" he asked, because why else would I show up at his job?

"No, just came to see you," I said, and that caused him to glance around, to see if anyone had overheard, but I'd said it in all innocence, with no undertone.

"Hang on," he said, and disappeared into the shop. He came back in a minute and walked past me, back toward the road, lighting a cigarette as he went. "Come on," he said, and I followed. When we were well enough away, he faced me and said, "Look, Danny, you can't come and see me like this at work. People already talk... and I don't need 'em talking about me like that."

I actually chuckled. I knew the things people said about me, and most of them were true: I was gay, and it showed, and people knew it. I'd been called faggot, fairy, sissy, fruit, queer most of my life. I didn't like it, but I couldn't change it. And I could understand why Rowdy didn't want to be called those names. No one wanted to be called those names. "That's not why I came to see you," I told him.

We stood by my car and Rowdy smoked his cigarette. "What then?" he asked me, squinting against the sun.

"I'm leaving tomorrow for Dallas," I said. "I start school in two weeks."

He grinned. "Well, look at you. Gettin' all fancy."

I ignored the sarcasm; I hadn't expected him to be impressed. "I just came to say goodbye." And I stood there for a long moment, trying to decide if I should offer my hand for him to shake, and if I did, would he even shake it? We had never hugged, despite all the times we'd had sex, but as we both stood there in that interminable and awkward silence, I wondered if we might now.

Rowdy smoked. "So tomorrow, huh?"

"Yeah."

He nodded, squinted at me, glanced off toward the garage. "That's good," he said. "Good for you."

"Yeah..." Then I put an end to it and stepped toward my car door, digging in my pocket for my keys. Instead of a handshake, instead of a hug, I put my hand on Rowdy's shoulder and he didn't flinch or step away. "Take care of yourself, Rowdy."

"Yeah," he said. "You, too."

And that was the last time I ever saw him.

Once I was up and showered and getting dressed for the wedding, I was seized with the urge to drive out to the old junkyard. I called Mama to ask if it was still there. "Lord, no," she said. "They cleaned all that up a while back and put in a little strip of stores out that way. And a storage place."

"It's all gone?" I asked, and my voiced cracked.

"The trailer's still there," she said, and it filled me with relief.

I drove out there, knowing I risked being late for Rhonda's wedding, but for some reason I didn't really care. She would be mad, but she would get over it; and I wouldn't be that late if I just drove out, saw the place, and drove back.

Mama was right. The junkyard was gone, replaced with a low budget shopping strip with a Family Dollar, a place called Karen's Kut 'n' Kurl, and a Chinese restaurant. A high, wooden fence separated the strip and it's parking lot from the trailer. I parked and stood staring at it in a kind of awe that it hadn't collapsed. There were children's playthings in the yard and an oak tree shaded it from the worst of the sun. From where I stood, I could hear the window air conditioner unit; someone was home. The sweet, greasy stink from the Chinese restaurant hung in the air.

Then I was walking toward it, pulled by the past. I wondered who lived there now, and I thought I might call Mama and see if she knew; she somehow managed to know everything about everyone. As I stepped around the fence, the front door opened and a little boy raced out and down the rickety wooden steps. "Austin!" came a woman's voice from inside.

I was suddenly nervous, like I'd been caught at something I shouldn't have been doing. I thought of going back to my car and driving on to the wedding, but something held me there, watching. The little boy ran to a bike on the ground under the tree just as the woman came out of the trailer, a baby on her hip, leading another child by the hand.

"Austin, I told you—" She saw me and stopped. Austin froze, half on the bike and half off. They all turned to me. "Can I help you?" She sounded slightly irritated, though whether with me for being there, peeping around the fence at them like some weirdo, or at Austin for disobeying.

"Oh, um..." I stepped around the fence and smiled to reassure her that I wasn't a pedophile or a rapist or whatever she might be thinking I was. "My friend used to live here," I heard myself say, because why not just get right to the point? "When we were kids..."

She sized me up—literally, looked me up and down—from where she stood in the door of the trailer. The baby squirmed but she held it firm. I couldn't tell if it was a boy or a girl. "You a preacher?"

That made me laugh. "No. I'm supposed to be at a wedding. I mean... I have a wedding later."

She squinted at me. "You're gonna be late to your own wedding?"

"Not me," I said. "I'm just the best man..."

She nodded, moved the baby to the other hip. "Oh. So you knew Rowdy when y'all was little?"

"Well, all the way up until high school, actually." I stepped closer. "My name's Danny. I used to live up the road, that way." I nodded back over my shoulder in the direction of where I used to live.

She considered my name for a second or two, then shook her head. "I don't remember him ever talking about anybody named Danny," she said, and even though I knew she didn't mean it that way, hearing it actually hurt my feelings just a bit.

"It was a long time ago," I said. "Almost thirty years." She nodded. I asked, "Are you his wife?"

It was her turn to laugh. "God, no. He wasn't really the kind to marry." I can't tell if she meant he wasn't the kind of man she *wanted* to marry, or if he simply wasn't interested in matrimony. "Did he seem like the kind who'd settle down?"

I shook my head, but I was seeing three children and the mother of them, so it seemed he'd settled down pretty well. "Are these his kids?" It was then I got a real good look at the one she'd called Austin; there was no way Rowdy could ever have denied that one.

It was like she'd read my mind. "Austin looks just damned like him, don't he?"

"Pretty much."

The boy blinked up at me, the spitting image of Rowdy. I guessed him to be about seven years old, a couple years younger than when I'd first met Rowdy, but it was clear he would grow into the same wiry, compact teen that his father had been. He probably had the same quick temper Rowdy had, too; then I corrected myself. Attitude is not genetic. If he turned out like Rowdy, it would be because of his circumstances and not because his father had been short-tempered.

"Hi," I said to him, but he didn't respond.

"You know what happened to him?" she asked me, and for a second I was confused because I thought she was talking about the boy; like, maybe he was deaf, and something had happened to him. Then I realized she meant Rowdy, of course. "Yeah," I said, and I felt my blood turn to ice. "Another friend told me all about it. It was awful."

She shrugged. "I can't say I didn't see it coming. You know? I mean, ain't we all told, all our lives, that when you get messed up in drugs and the people that use them, you pretty much get what you deserve? Well, I told him that and told him that, but he was stubborn as a mule. You knew him."

I nodded. "Yeah..." I wouldn't say stubborn, though. Rowdy was resigned to his fate, so basically anything that led to the dead end he had accepted for himself, and selling drugs was one of those things. "Was it meth?"

She nodded. "I don't know where he was making it, though. The cops come by here a bunch of times—they knew he was dealing it, they just couldn't never catch him—but they never found anything here." She shrugged again. I had a feeling she did a lot of shrugging in her life. "I was always scared for him, but he said he had everything under control..."

"I just can't believe he got in the car with them," I said, thinking out loud more than anything. "He had to know…"

"I said the same thing," she said, "but he said he needed to get the money, and he said they were just a bunch of stupid kids." She paused. "He usually has his gun on him, too, but he didn't take it that night. I don't know why…" She shifted the baby to her other hip. "Do you wanna come inside?" She was probably asking because she wanted to sit down and stop holding that child.

I had wanted nothing more than to see where Rowdy lived, back when it was surrounded by the magical landscape of that vanished junkyard, but now that I had the chance, I knew I wouldn't take it before the words were even out of my mouth. "Thanks, but no. I need to be going or I'm going to miss the wedding." And I started backing away, toward where I'd parked the rental car. Rowdy's son watched me go.

"What did you say your name was again?" she called to me.

"Danny."

"Well, thank you, Danny," she said, and I guessed because it was good for her to talk about it and get some things off her chest.

"You're welcome." And just before I went around the fence, I turned back. "Where is he buried?"

She pointed. "If you drive back the way you came, turn right at the stop light instead of left, then go about half a mile. Cemetery's on the left, across from the church."

I followed her directions, ignoring the calls and texts from Rhonda. The church was easy to find, and Rowdy's was the freshest grave in the cemetery across the road. I don't know why I felt it was important to see it. Maybe to finally cut whatever tie had bound us for so long, but when I stood over the sparkling new headstone, I thought there must be some mistake.

MAYNARD WILSON was the name inscribed there, and I thought I had some much older man's grave, then it hit me: Rowdy was a nickname, of course. I probably wouldn't have gone by Maynard, either. And the dates were right. This was Rowdy's grave.

I stood for maybe a minute before I felt dumb for even being there, so I turned back toward the rental car. "You should have gotten out of here, Rowdy," I said, softly, over my shoulder to his grave as I walked away.

In the car, I texted Rhonda: *On my way. Long story.*

Then I pulled away from the church, and it struck me that I had forgotten to ask the woman who was the mother of Rowdy's kids her name.

Decoration Day

Uncle Vernon didn't die in the war. He came back, a pretty Vietnamese bride on his arm, and went to work at the mill, like everyone else. Nobody made much of a fuss over him; there was no hero's parade down Center Street, though Aunt June did cook a big dinner for him, and a bunch of people from the church came. Other than that, he and his wife moved into a trailer back behind Aunt June and Uncle Alvin's place, and he started at the mill that following week. He lived three more years before he died, and that's when people started acting differently about him.

Tammy was five years old when he came back from Vietnam, and all she really remembered was the long car ride to Birmingham in the back seat of Uncle Alvin's Continental, sandwiched between her aunts June and Nadine while they chain smoked. She was eight when he died, so she remembered more. It happened at night, and she was awakened, not by her mother telling her the bad news, but by the ghastly wailing of Auntie Kim, Vernon's wife. The trailer was at the back of the property, almost in the woods, but Tammy could hear it as clear as if Auntie Kim were in the next room. It had terrified her. She remembered that most of all.

She remembered the funeral, too, parts of it. The flowers, and the framed portrait of Uncle Vernon sitting atop the closed casket. She'd asked her mother why the casket was closed, but all her mother said was "Shhh," so she didn't ask again. She remembered Auntie Kim was silent, in stark contrast to the wailing she'd done upon receiving the news of her husband's death. And she seemed smaller, too. Tammy was tall for her age, and she was almost as tall as Auntie Kim.

"Bless her heart," Tammy's mother said, and shook her head.

Tammy looked at the back of Auntie Kim's head, then at Aunt June, who was inconsolable, across the aisle. She guessed Auntie Kim had gotten all her grief out that first night, then she started wishing the funeral would hurry up and end. She was hungry, and she hated wearing dresses.

Mama told her to leave Auntie Kim in peace, to mind her own business and let the woman grieve. "How would you feel if you'd just lost your husband and no one would leave you alone?" her mother asked.

Tammy couldn't say. She couldn't imagine being married, much less being a widow. She didn't even like boys. She promised to leave Auntie Kim alone, and it was easy at first because she had school, but when summer started she had more time to notice that she hadn't seen her aunt since the funeral.

"Maybe she's dead, too," her cousin Randall said. They were patching the back tire on Tammy's bike.

She slapped him, hard, on the shoulder.

"Ow!"

"Don't say that!"

"Well, where's she at, then? It's like she disappeared or something!"

They speculated at length about what might have happened to Auntie Kim: had she gone back to Vietnam? "I doubt that," Tammy said. "She's American now, ain't she? They'd probably kill her over there." She had only a vague concept of Vietnam, and that from snatches of the news and conversations between the grown-ups she had overheard. There had been a war—Uncle Vernon had left right out of high school to go fight in it—but she didn't understand why he'd gone, other than to fight the Communists, but not the Russians. Apparently, there were other Communists, and they must have won the war, which made no sense, because Uncle Alvin and Aunt June were always carrying on about what a hero Uncle Vernon had been. And Tammy couldn't help but wonder: if Uncle Vernon and the American soldiers were such heroes, how had the Communists won?

"Maybe they came here and kidnapped her," Randall suggested.

He and Tammy had climbed the old oak tree in the field next to Tammy's house and were lounging in its shade. It was hot already, and it was barely the middle of April. They reclined against the gnarled branches, their feet swinging. Randall dozed. Tammy stared across the road and past Alvin and June's house to Auntie Kim's trailer.

"Maybe she moved," Randall said, out of the blue.

Tammy hoped not. "Where would she move to?"

Randall shrugged as well as he could in his position. "Maybe she has some family somewhere," he said. "Like California. There's a lot of Chinese people in California."

Tammy rolled her eyes, even though her cousin couldn't see it. "Stupid. She's not Chinese, she's Vietnamese."

"Same difference."

Tammy didn't even bother to correct him, she just went back to watching for Auntie Kim to appear and hoping there wasn't something wrong.

She saw her that following weekend. Tammy was riding her bike and practicing doing it with no hands so Randall would stop making fun of her because she was afraid she would wreck. It was a stretch of road with no houses, so she thought she'd try it. She'd decided she just about had the hang of it and was feeling pretty good about herself, when she rounded a corner and there was Auntie Kim walking along the shoulder of the road in a yellow sundress and red sandals, swinging a big straw hat.

Tammy was so surprised to see her there that she lost focus of riding with no hands, then lost control of the bike. The front wheel turned sharply, pitching her over the handlebars and planting her on the cracked asphalt of the road. The noise she made when she landed made Auntie Kim turn, her mouth a perfect circle of astonishment. "Oh!"

Tammy's knees and palms felt like they were on fire. She got to her feet as fast as she could, because she didn't want to look stupid in front of Auntie Kim. She even threw the bike a look of derision where it lay half in the weeds on the side of the road, its front tire spinning idiotically.

"Tammy?" Auntie Kim was running toward her, her tiny feet in their red sandals tapping out a rhythm of panic. "Are you hurt?"

"No," Tammy lied.

"You are bleeding!"

"I'll be fine."

"You come with me." And Auntie Kim took her by the hand. Tammy was so relieved to know that Auntie Kim was all right, that she hadn't moved away or worse, that she was willing to be led away, but she remembered her bike and ran back for it.

Not much had changed about the interior of the trailer. Tammy guessed she'd expected it to have been converted to a shrine to Uncle Vernon and his memory, but everything was basically the same as she remembered from the few times she'd visited when he was still alive. The only traces of Uncle Vernon that she saw were a photograph of him in his dress uniform, taken a week before he left for the war, and a tiny framed photograph on top of the television set.

She couldn't make out the details but she knew it could only be a picture of them together—Uncle Vernon and Auntie Kim—probably the day they were married, so that meant it was taken in Vietnam. She wanted to go closer and see it better, but she needed to sit still while her scrapes were cleaned.

"How you did this?" Kim asked, washing one skinned knee with warm water and Ivory soap. She was so gentle it didn't even sting.

"I just came around that curve and lost control," Tammy lied. She shrugged for added effect. "Maybe I hit a rock or something in the road."

"It is not so bad." Kim inspected her handiwork. Tammy noticed for the first time that there was a light spray of freckles across the bridge of her nose. "You lucky." She wrung the washcloth out and reached for Tammy's hand. "You be more careful next time."

She clenched her teeth against the stinging when the soap met the raw flesh of her palm. "What's that picture?" She nodded to the photograph on the TV set.

Kim turned toward it. "Our wedding," she said, simply, and returned to nursing Tammy's palms.

"Was that in Vietnam?"

Auntie Kim nodded. "Just before Saigon fall." She paused, then corrected herself. "*Fell*." She started on the other palm, picking out the bits of gravel with her tiny fingertips.

215

"Were you scared?" Tammy asked. She'd seen the footage on the news, people gathered on top of a building as a helicopter took off with people dangling from it. She would have been terrified.

"War is very scary," Auntie Kim said, simply. "Always. But I am happy to be here now."

Tammy could understand that. "Do you miss him? Uncle Vernon?"

Auntie Kim bathed her knee, then she smiled. "No," she said. "He has not left me."

For a second, Tammy wasn't sure she'd heard correctly. Then she thought Auntie Kim might be speaking metaphorically, which they'd covered in her English class before the Easter break; like when Aunt Nadine said "Vernon may be gone, but he's still with us in spirit."

"I miss him, too," she said, because she'd heard so many people say that at the funeral, she guessed it was the proper thing to say. She hadn't really known her uncle that well. She was so young when he'd left for the war and not much older when he'd come back. She remembered him as young and handsome and laughing, at least before he left. In the photograph on top of the television set, she could see that he was smiling. That was clear.

"He visits me," Auntie Kim said, still smiling. "We talk."

A chill crept up Tammy's spine then, and she didn't know what to say.

She thought a lot about what Auntie Kim had said, about Uncle Vernon visiting her and talking with her, and it both thrilled and concerned her. She believed in ghosts and always had—not because she'd seen one with her own eyes, but because she felt if she believed, then she would surely be visited by one, and sooner rather than later. She would be nine soon, and she'd already stopped believing in Santa Claus, the Easter bunny, and the Tooth Fairy; if she was going to keep believing in ghosts, she needed one to show up soon or she could promise nothing.

Maybe I'll see Uncle Vernon's ghost, she thought, then chided herself for wishing such a thing. Auntie Kim probably hadn't seen him, either. She probably just meant that she sits alone in her trailer and talks to Uncle Vernon, even though he wasn't really there and she knew that. People did that when they were grieving. People also talked to God, and she was pretty sure he never showed himself, either.

"I can't imagine what she does all day, cooped up like that," Mama said one night after dinner.

"Bless her heart," Aunt June said, and lit a cigarette.

"Reckon what she's gonna do," Aunt Nadine said. "Long term, I mean. She can't spend the rest of her life in that trailer."

"It ain't even been a year," June pointed out. "Give her some time."

They lapsed into silence for a moment. Tammy washed the dishes with her back to them, pretended not to be listening, but hanging on every word. Her aunts and her mother were busybodies sometimes; she hoped they would leave Auntie Kim alone.

"Reckon she'll stay here or go back to Vietnam?" Mama asked. She said each syllable and rhymed the last one with *yam:* Vi-et-NAM. Tammy had to make herself not correct her mother.

June and Nadine seemed nonplussed. "Why in the world would she want to go back?" Nadine asked.

"Well, she's from there," Mama said. "If it was you, and you were there, wouldn't you want to come back here?"

June sniffed. "I don't even see how you can compare here with there," she said.

Tammy couldn't stay silent any longer. "She's not going back to Vietnam," she told them, over her shoulder without turning. "She likes it here. She said so." The three women fell silent, and Tammy stole a look at them over her shoulder as she rinsed a glass.

"And how do you know?" asked Mama.

"She told me," Tammy said with a shrug. "I had a wreck on my bike and she cleaned me up and we talked about it." She drained the sink, hung the damp dishcloth on the faucet, and turned to face them, fully expecting them to berate her for bothering Auntie Kim like that.

"Well, how did she look?" Nadine asked.

"Does she need anything?" June wanted to know.

"Is she okay?" Mama asked.

Tammy shrugged again. "She's okay, I guess. She said she misses Uncle Vernon." She was not about to make any mention of what Auntie Kim had said about him visiting her.

"Well, bless her heart," Aunt June said again, and lit another cigarette.

Now that she'd been once, Tammy wasn't so hesitant to visit Auntie Kim, and it meant she had less time to spend with Randall, pretending not to be offended when he talked about sex, which seemed to be the only thing on his mind anymore. She would never understand boys, not if she lived a million years.

"Do ever want to go back to Vietnam?" she asked Auntie Kim one afternoon. They were sitting on opposite ends of the couch. Auntie Kim was working on a piece of elaborate embroidery and Tammy was watching TV, waiting for *General Hospital* to come on.

"Sometimes, I think... maybe I can go back there," Kim said, without looking up from her needlework. She didn't wear glasses, and how she could achieve such detail astounded Tammy. "But I like America more than I miss Vietnam." The way she said it made the way everyone else pronounce it sound vulgar. "Here I am safe. There is no war."

On the television, Monica Quartermaine confronted her husband, who she suspected was having an affair with Lesley Webber. Tammy asked Auntie Kim, "When you said Uncle Vernon still came to see you? And that y'all talked?"

Auntie Kim embroidered. "Yes?"

"What did you mean?"

She looked up, her needle poised in the air. "You think I do not tell the truth." If she was insulted or angered by Tammy's question, she gave no sign of it and went back to her embroidery.

"No, no," Tammy said, and leaned forward, like her posture would help convince Auntie Kim. "I don't think you're lying. I just wanted to know. You said he visited you..."

Auntie Kim nodded slowly.

"Like, every night?"

"No, but many times..."

Tammy was intrigued. She leaned closer. "What's it like? When he visits you?"

Auntie Kim stopped embroidering, folded her hands in her lap and looked at Tammy. "The first time, I am afraid." She paused as she searched for the right words to use. "In my country, we do not believe in ghosts the way you do here, in America." She paused, sighed, then went on: "In my country, when someone dies peacefully and the proper rituals are done, they do not become a *ghost*, but join all our ancestors. They help the family when we call on them and give them offerings. But if someone dies and—" Here she paused again and looked away. Tammy noticed that her fists were clenched in her lap.

"You don't have to talk about it if you don't want," Tammy said. She felt bad, coming here and making Auntie Kim relive all the pain she'd endured since Uncle Vernon's death.

"I did not give Vernon what he needs in the..." Her brow furrowed as she searched her brain for the word. "... The other world, the one after life. I wasn't able to. I asked June and Nadine and they told me he didn't need them, that here, they are unnecessary." She fixed Tammy with a firm stare. "But they are necessary and I did not know what to do and now Vernon can not be at peace." Another pause. Auntie Kim stared down at her hands. "We call them *ma đói*. The ghosts who are not at peace. I want Vernon to be at peace."

Tammy wanted it, too, suddenly. More than anything she had ever wanted in her life, and for no other reason than her aunt's distress over it. She didn't understand, really, but she wanted her uncle to be at peace on the other side and stop visiting Auntie Kim.

"But, here," Kim continued, after a long moment in which she just stared at the needlework in her lap, "I do not know how. In my country, we have..." And her voice trailed off as she searched her mind for the right word. "In English, it would be like... a medium?" She is still not sure of the word.

"Like someone who reads cards?" Tammy asked. "Like a fortune teller?" She really couldn't see where this was leading at all.

"Yes!" Auntie Kim was suddenly excited. She set her embroidery aside and leaned forward in her chair, grabbed Tammy's arm. "Is there someone like this here?"

"Yeah...," Tammy told her, "but... Well, it's just old Virgie that lives up the road from us. She's about a hundred years old and she ain't got any teeth. She dips, too."

Auntie Kim stood up. "Take me to her?"

Tammy stood, too, still uncertain about everything. "Okay," she said reluctantly.

They walked there. Tammy had to almost jog to keep up with the woman, who she'd never seen move so fast in the time she'd known her. And she kept looking back over her shoulder to make sure Mama or one of her other aunts weren't following them. Mama would skin her alive if she found her at Virgie's. "Devil mess," she called what the old woman did, and Tammy wasn't entirely sure she didn't believe that herself.

The woman lived in a house that looked like it had fallen in twenty years ago but the inhabitants had forgotten to evacuate. There was bright green moss growing on the sagging roof, and kudzu blanketed the entire left side of the structure, such that it was.

Virgie sat on the porch in a metal chair and watched them approach from the road. She spat as they reached the stoop, sized them both up, said, "You're Vernon Dickey's wife, ain't you?"

"Yes, ma'am," Auntie Kim answered, very polite. She even bowed.

Virgie turned to Tammy and grinned her toothless, tobacco-stained grin. "Won't your mama tear the hide off you if she knows you're here, missy?"

Tammy turned scarlet. "She don't know we're here," she said, so nervous that her voice sounded pinched in the back of her mouth.

Virgie laughed. "You wouldn't be here if she did," she said, then looked to the older of the two. "You'll be wanting my help, though."

"My husband," Auntie Kim said.

Virgie nodded and heaved herself up and out of her chair with a grunt. "Come on inside, then," she said, and held the screen door open for the woman. To Tammy she said, "You wait here."

Tammy was both relieved and disappointed. Mama always said Virgie was a witch, and Tammy had wanted to see inside her house, where Randall assured her there were body parts in jars everywhere, even though he had never been inside himself. But he had heard.

So she sat on the steps until she got scared there could be something lurking under the woman's house that might reach between them and grab her by the ankle and drag her to her death, then she moved up and sat cross-legged on the porch. She strained her ears to hear what Virgie might be saying to Auntie Kim, but could hear nothing over the sounds of the insects in the high weeds that surrounded the porch. She expected she was going to be there a while and wished she had something to occupy her time, like a magazine or a book. She would have been glad for Randall's company, even.

Then the door opened and Auntie Kim stepped out, smiling. "Thank you, Miss Virgie," she said, and gave another small bow. "Very much."

Virgie just grunted and settled herself back in her rusty chair. "Y'all better get on, before your mama finds out. Or I turn you into frogs or something." She laughed and showed her toothless gums, the inside of her mouth stained by her tobacco.

The sight revolted Tammy. She let Auntie Kim take her by the arm and lead her back to the road.

Later, back in Auntie Kim's trailer, they burned incense and drew pictures of things on paper. Tammy was perplexed at first, but she suspected it all had something to do with Vernon's death and what Virgie had told her aunt in secret. "Can you draw a car?" Auntie Kim asked her.

Tammy blinked. "I... I think so. I never tried."

Auntie Kim thrust paper and pencil toward her. "Try."

Uncle Vernon had driven a Lincoln Continental, and Tammy and Randall had called it "The Batmobile." It was long and black and sleek in ways that neither could name, and they always asked for a ride whenever they could. Uncle Vernon always obliged, and they had felt like royalty as he crept slowly along the back roads and through the streets of town, sure that everyone was staring, envious.

She tried to recreate the Lincoln—now as gone as Uncle Vernon was; Auntie Kim had sold it after his death—though she knew she would never do it justice. Afterward, she sat back from her handiwork, frowned at its dubious quality. "I don't know," she said.

Auntie Kim picked it up and smiled. "It is very good," she said. "You are very talented."

Tammy smiled though she knew better. "I could probably do it better with practice."

"This will be fine." Auntie Kim added it to her own pile: drawings of clothes, of a bed, of shoes. "In my country," she explained, "we would buy these things. Little clothes, a little bed, shoes, a car... a bicycle. All made of paper. But here, we must make them ourselves." She handed Tammy more paper. "Can you draw a fishing pole? And a tackle box?"

Tammy did her best. "What are these for?" she asked.

"For Vernon," Auntie Kim explained.

"I figured that, but how are they for Uncle Vernon? And why? Is it because of what old Virgie told you?"

The woman looked up and her brow furrowed. The sight of it actually surprised Tammy just a bit; Auntie Kim's skin was always so smooth and flawless. "Tammy, what does it mean, a *decoration day?*"

"That's what old people call Memorial Day," Tammy explained. "It's when you decorate the graves of the people who served in the wars. Like Uncle Vernon and Pawpaw. It's in a couple weeks, actually."

Auntie Kim nodded. "Okay. Here is what we must do." Then she leaned in and whispered her plan to Tammy.

When she had finished, Tammy said, "Aunt June's gonna shit a brick!" But she was grinning because she liked the idea, so she agreed to help Auntie Kim.

When Tammy was little, maybe four, and Mama said it was Decoration Day, so they were going to go to the cemetery and decorate Papaw's grave, Tammy was thrilled. She pictured something like Christmas, only in May. Was there a tree for Decoration Day, or could they use the ceramic one that plugged in? There was nowhere to plug it at the cemetery, though. Maybe they could take the bulb out and use a candle.

She dressed in her best dress—it was long and the fabric looked like it was made from a patchwork quilt and it was trimmed with lace—and went down to the basement to dig out the ceramic tree and a string or two of silver garland. It was frayed a bit in several places, but she thought no one would notice if she hung a few glass balls in the bare spots. She chose blue and green and red, which was less like Christmas and more like summer, she guessed.

Upstairs, she presented the box of decorations to her mother and Aunt June. "What's this for?" Aunt June asked, and scowled at the collection in the box.

"Mama said we was decorating Papaw's grave," Tammy explained, proud of herself, "so I got the decorations."

Mama laughed, then Aunt June laughed, and Tammy laughed, too, at first. Then she realized they were laughing at her and she started to cry. "Oh, honey, stop crying," Mama said, and handed her a paper towel off the roll. "You didn't know no better."

"I just wanted to make it look nice," Tammy snuffled, and wiped her eyes.

"I know, honey, but we decorate the graves with *flowers* on Decoration Day, and *flags*. Not Christmas decorations."

Aunt June held up a bouquet of red, white, and blue flowers—carnations and chrysanthemums and mums—with an American flag protruding from the top. Tammy leaned in and smelled the flowers but decided she didn't like them. They didn't smell like roses or even the daisies she picked alongside the road. These flowers smelled like they were on the verge of rot, and she decided that must be what a grave smelled like.

In the car, Aunt June was inconsolable in the front seat and Aunt Nadine just sat and stared out the window. "He was so *young*," June kept saying. Tammy sat with Auntie Kim and Aunt Nadine in the back seat and felt embarrassed for Aunt June.

She cut a sidelong glance at Auntie Kim, who sat composed with her hands on the bag filled with incense and the decorations they had made. Aunt June was acting like she was the one who'd been married to Uncle Vernon.

"You want some gum, Tammy?" Aunt Nadine asked, and proffered a stick of Juicy Fruit.

Tammy took it, but didn't put it in her mouth. In the front seat, Aunt June wailed like a banshee. When they'd picked her up, Tammy smelled liquor when Aunt June got in the car. She knew it was liquor because that was how Uncle Alvin smelled all the time, and everyone knew he drank. *Like a fish,* as Aunt June liked to say. So maybe it was the liquor that was making Aunt June act like she'd lost her mind. Tammy decided to just ignore it.

Mama parked in the church lot, which was packed, and they walked up the hill to the cemetery. Grass had finally started to grow over Uncle Vernon's grave, but it was still the freshest grave there. Mama removed the old flowers from the urns to either side of the headstone and replaced them with the fresh ones they'd brought—red, white, and blue carnations. Aunt June and Aunt Nadine inserted little American flags and they all stood back to admire their handiwork.

Tammy knew better than to point out that Uncle Vernon had not died while serving, and neither had Papaw, so technically they didn't need to decorate the graves at all, but she knew how important this was to her mother and her aunts. She stood quietly between Mama and Aunt June, who continued to cry into a handful of Kleenex, waiting for Auntie Kim to step forward to perform the ritual they'd discussed and realizing she was so anxious about it she was shaking.

And as she waited for Auntie Kim to do something, she realized just how pointless the whole thing was. Mama and her aunts talked and talked about it, their anticipation for the day as palpable as a child's with Christmas or the circus. Flowers—always red, white, and blue carnations or mums—and miniature flags were purchased. There was a church service on Sunday, then on Monday they drove out to the cemetery to Papaw's grave. Now, in the wake of Uncle Vernon's death, there was an added note of gravity to the day, but nothing more. No one recited a poem, no one said a prayer or sang a hymn. The flowers were placed and everyone just stood there.

"Now what?" Tammy asked it aloud, but she hadn't meant to. She turned scarlet and Mama threw her a look.

Aunt June wiped her nose and looked off into the distance. "Let's go find Daddy's," she said, like no one knew where it was and they would have to spread out to search.

That was when Auntie Kim took something from her purse, shook it out, and placed it atop her head. Tammy had watched her make it—a white hood, worn by mourners in Vietnam—but the initial sight of it still took her slightly aback. "Tammy? Will you help me?"

They had rehearsed it this way, so she knew what to do, but having Mama there made it less easy. She knew better than to ask permission, she doubted she would get it; she also knew that if she didn't just do as they'd practiced, she would probably chicken out. So, she took the incense and placed it around Uncle Vernon's headstone.

"What in the entire hell...?" Aunt June sounded far away.

So did Mama when she said, "Shh."

Tammy lit the incense and the smell of jasmine filled the air. Auntie Kim prayed softly, words in a language so foreign to Tammy that it might as well have been made up.

"What is she doing?" Aunt June hissed.

"Putting him to rest, looks like," Aunt Nadine said, and Aunt June grunted. Mama said nothing and Tammy did not dare turn to see the looks on their faces.

It was over quickly. For some reason, Tammy had imagined it taking time, but Auntie Kim had offered each tiny, paper thing they'd made to Vernon's spirit, burned it, then moved on to the next item. The whole ritual took less than five minutes, then she removed her hood, folded it neatly, and put it into her purse. "Thank you," she said to Tammy, and to the women, "Thank you."

No one said anything, they just turned in the direction of Papaw's grave. Tammy followed along behind them, the scent of that jasmine incense lingering in her nostrils, or maybe it was following them. Maybe Uncle Vernon was in the incense and he didn't want them to go, so he trailed them in the smoke. Tammy quickened her pace to catch up with Mama and her aunts, just in case Auntie Kim's ritual hadn't worked.

Somebody's Always Saying Goodbye

1.

Steven found out he was dying when he turned thirty-five and was still filled with hope and determination, so while his doctor said words like *glioblastoma* and *astrocytoma* and *secondary*, Steven just sat there, because he was dying and he wasn't sure what else to do, and while he had suspected as much himself, hearing it spoken gave it substance.

I'm going to die, he thought.

"The good news," his doctor said, and actually smiled, "is that yours is a less aggressive anaplastic astrocytoma." That word again. Steven pictured stars, constellations, galaxies. "Prognosis is much better."

"How long, then?" he asked the doctor, who he guessed was his age. This doctor had years and years left; he would marry, father children, travel the world, retire. He would die peacefully in his sleep, ninety-something-years-old, surrounded by sons and daughters and grandchildren who had his ears, his chin, his nose.

"Two to three years."

Steven actually laughed. Or, rather, he made a sound that would have to pass for a laugh from a man who had just learned he had two to three years left to live. Honestly, he had expected it to be considerably less. Weeks, maybe months. "And that is without treatment?" he asked.

"That is after surgery and a regimen of chemotherapy or radiation."

Steven nodded. *I'm going to die,* he thought again.

He did not die, though.

He called his parents and they flew in from Sonoma. His sister drove down from Charleston and his brother, on assignment in Sydney, could not apologize enough for not being able to come in. They helped him in the days leading up to the surgery and with his convalescence, and when he was able to get around on his own, he assured them they could all go back home, that he would be fine.

"You call us if you need *anything,* you hear me?" His mother gripped his arm tight and would not let go until he swore a vow. He would call, he promised, no matter what time of day or night, if he needed anything at all.

His father clapped him on the shoulder, as if he'd just kicked a field goal and won a championship, but gently. "You take care of yourself," the man said, brusque, which is how fathers are because they believe this gruffness, like that of a bear, will keep the cancer at bay.

"I will, Dad," Steven said.

His sister hugged him and then they were all gone. He was actually relieved, and felt a quick stab of guilt. They were only trying to help, he understood that, but it was nice to have his apartment to himself again. To celebrate, he took a shower and walked around naked afterward. It was the simple things.

Several days later there was a soft knock on his door, and since he was still walking around naked any chance he got, he threw on his robe and peered through the peephole. He could barely see the top of a head, the hair wild and perhaps reddish. He suspected a child selling something for school, but he was surprised when he opened the door and saw his neighbor from downstairs. He knew her name—Mrs. Zitler—but they both kept to themselves, so they had never spoken.

"Mrs. Zitler!" Steven searched his mind for any possible reason why she would knock on his door. Maybe just to borrow some sugar, or an egg, or maybe she had a petition for him to sign. Did people still borrow sugar like that, he wondered?

"Hello," she said, then the two of them stood there in silence. Steven wondered if she'd forgotten why she'd knocked; like, perhaps she had dementia and had mistaken his door for her own.

"Can I help you with something?" he asked finally, when the silence was too much to bear.

"I spoke with your mother," Mrs. Zitler replied and blinked up at him from behind her eyeglasses, which were too large for her face. "When she was here? You were in hospital and she asked of me that I would check in on you." A pause. "From time to time."

"Oh, yeah," Steven said, and pretended that he had known all along, though his mother had said nothing to him about assigning Mrs. Zitler this task. "Would you like to come in?" He held the door open, but she shook her head.

"No, no. I must not stay. I have only come to see that you are well." She smiled, and Steven smiled back. "And you are well, yes?"

"I am well, yes, thank you."

"Good," she said. And again, "Good. Then the cancer, it is gone?"

Steven considered that. He'd had surgery and his first round of radiation. The cancer was as gone as it could be at that point, so he told Mrs. Zitler that.

"Good," she said again. Then: "I will leave you now. Goodbye."

"Goodbye, Mrs. Zitler." He closed the door on her back as she made her way back down the hallway to the stairwell. He made a mental note to mention Mrs. Zitler to his mother the next time they talked; surely she had not meant for the woman to check on him, but apparently Mrs. Zitler had taken her literally. Of course, by the time he spoke to his mother again, he forgot to question her about it, because that happened sometimes after you had a brain tumor removed. You forgot things.

235

Steven didn't die, but his father did, of a heart attack one day while mowing the lawn. His sister delivered the news, and Steven booked a flight to Sonoma between treatments. He spent the entire weekend telling people about his surgery. "Honestly, it hasn't been as bad as I expected." They pressed him for details, and he was as polite as he could be, until he finally just had to tell people, "We're here for my mother. Let's just concentrate on the shivah."

"They're just concerned for you, Steven," his mother whispered to him.

"I'm fine, though." And really, he was, considering. "We should be talking about Dad. They can all sit around and cluck over me like a bunch of old hens when it's my shivah."

His mother was so taken aback by what he'd said that she had to excuse herself from the room. Everyone seemed to understand, and Steven sat surrounded by the men and women who had been his parents' friends, wishing he could think of something else he might do instead. He couldn't settle on anything that hadn't already been taken care of.

"Your mother tells us you have brain cancer," said one man. Steven couldn't think of his name, but he thought it might be one of his father's cousins. His voice carried to every corner of the house and people turned to see.

Steven nodded and rubbed his palms on his jeans. "Yeah," he said.

"How are you feeling, then? You look pretty good."

236

He shrugged. "I feel pretty good, I guess." Then he thought of something he could do, and he stood. "I'm going to check the mail. Excuse me." And as he left the room, he heard the man's wife admonish him, her voice like the hisses of a cat.

His sister drove him to the airport for his flight home. "Sorry about everybody," she said. "I wish there was something I could have done, but you know how people are."

He shrugged. "I have brain cancer. What can I say?" And for about half a second, the most acute dread blossomed in the center of his chest, and he had to stop to catch his breath. *I have brain cancer. I'm going to die.* There were actually moments—days, even—when he forgot. His sister panicked, of course.

"Oh my God, Steven, are you okay?"

"Yes," he said, and realized he was actually holding his breath as he waited for the terror to pass. *I'm going to die,* he told himself again. He let his breath out slowly and took a tentative couple of steps. "I'm fine."

"Don't scare me like that," she said, and gripped his arm tight. "Especially not after this weekend."

"Sorry," he said. "I just forget I'm dying sometimes. Then I remember. It's scary."

His sister had no response, and so they walked on in silence.

Mrs. Zitler met him at the door to their apartment building. "Hi," he said, and stepped around her.

"You are alive," she said.

Steven laughed. "Yeah. For now, I guess."

Mrs. Zitler did not laugh. "I knocked, and there was no answer. I came back later, and still there was no answer. I came back again, and again, and again. There was no answer, so I think you are maybe dead." She shrugged, as if to say, *What other possible conclusion could I have reached?* "So I am thinking I will call the police, but I look out my window and it is you, in a cab, and you are alive." Then she smiled. "This is good news."

He felt like he owed her an explanation. "I am *so* sorry, Mrs. Zitler, but my dad died, and my sister called, and I just ran out to catch the first flight I could, so I didn't have time to tell you." It occurred to him then that she had really taken his mother seriously, that she was to check on him regularly, like it was her job. "I'm really sorry."

"*Alav ha-Shalom,*" she said.

"Thank you."

"May his memory be for a blessing." Then Mrs. Zitler turned to go upstairs, but turned back and said, "And, please, you must call me Dora. My husband is gone twenty years now, and 'Mrs. Zitler' sounds—" Here she paused to think for a second, then finished: "—like an old lady."

Steven nodded. "Okay."

2.

They became friends.

Dora brought him food—kugels, matzoh ball soup, roast chicken; fattening things he would have turned his nose up at before, but something in her manner when she presented them to him made him relent. His treatments often left him nauseated, and she never pressed him to eat it in front of her, but she always seemed to know when he arrived home from a round of chemo or radiation, because fifteen minutes later, there was a knock at the door and there she was with a covered dish. "I bring you food," she always said, and Steven always accepted it and thanked her and invited her in.

When she started dusting once, and he insisted that she was a guest, she should sit, her response was to wave the cloth at him, like she was swatting at a bee, and told him, "You rest. I don't mind."

"But I mind," he said.

She waved the cloth at him again and continued to dust.

True, he barely had the energy to sit up, much less to clean. And it wasn't really that dirty, since he mostly watched TV from the sofa or lay in bed to read. Otherwise, he was at work, where he was assigned "light duty," which meant he stayed behind the counter and either rang up sales or directed people to the books they sought or to someone else who could help them locate or order it.

"You're sure you're up for this?" asked Janine, his boss.

"I'm good, really," he assured her. "The treatments just take a lot out of me. Once I get them out of the way, I'll be good as ever." He absently rubbed the scar over his right ear, which was turning into a habit since his hair fell out and he couldn't finger his curls the way he used to.

Janine smiled. "Okay," she said. "Good."

At home later, Steven panicked because he thought Janine might be planning to fire him. He replayed their conversation over and over again in his mind—him returning to work and explaining that he could only perform light duty, so maybe the register; Janine asking him if he was up to it, and him assuring her that he was. But had she been saying something else without actually saying it? Did she not think he was up for it, and asking it the way she had was her way of giving him the opportunity to admit it so she wouldn't have to let him go?

He felt a pain in his gut more acute than any nausea he might suffer after chemo or radiation, like he might vomit, and on top of that his heart was pounding so hard he could feel it in his earlobes and behind his eyes. His breath came in quick, tiny gasps. He wondered, too, if he might be dying, that somehow the cancer had made it to his lungs and his heart, and Janine had been able to see it manifested somehow, something he had missed.

He held his breath and waited to die. Then he didn't die, and he didn't vomit, and his heart rate returned to normal and his breathing settled and he sat on the floor and cried, relieved. Then he laughed, because it was funny that he should be relieved that he wasn't dying, when he *was* dying, only slowly.

There was a knock at the door. He wiped his face and answered it. It was Dora. She smiled and asked if he was hungry. "I made cabbage rolls," she said, and presented the plate to him.

3.

He did not die then, and he did not die the next month, or the next, or the next. Then he stopped counting the days and the weeks and the months. He finished his radiation treatments, then waited to begin chemotherapy.

Janine did not fire him, and they laughed about it over a beer one night after work. "You seriously thought I was thinking of firing you?" she asked. "You think I'm that kind of asshole? Come on!"

"Well, I wasn't sure," he confessed. The beer was his first since he'd begun radiation, and it tasted sour. He didn't remember beer tasting like that, and he wasn't too sure he'd be able to finish it. "I've never had cancer."

Janine laughed, a huge guffaw that made Steven laugh, too. They were still laughing when Janine's partner, Molly, joined them. She smiled at them as they laughed. "What did I miss?" she asked.

"Nothing, really," Janine told her, and wiped at her eyes.

"I have cancer," Steven said, and they laughed again, leaving Molly perplexed.

They settled down and Steven went to the bathroom where his reflection, as he washed his hands, still managed to startle him. The hair, mainly. He'd always allowed it to grow wild, only trimming it about twice a year. Now it was gone, the scar at his temple a livid purple still, and there were dark circles around his eyes. The sight of himself exhausted him, actually, and he decided he would go back to tell Janine and Molly that he was calling it a night.

They were deep in conversation when he returned, huddled together like they were planning a crime, their brows furrowed. "Well, did you even ask him?" he heard Molly ask.

"No," was Janine's answer. "It doesn't feel right just yet."

Molly rolled her eyes and was ready to say more, and Steven was tempted to ask what they were discussing since he was certain it was him, but he just said, "I think I'm gonna head out."

"You okay?" Janine asked, her concern genuine.

"I'm good," he said. "Just tired."

"Need a ride?"

He shook his head. "I'll catch a cab, but thanks."

They hugged, which was something he'd never really enjoyed, but since his diagnosis people seemed not to care whether he did or not. Janine's embrace lingered, like if she released him too soon there might be consequences neither of them could foresee. "Be careful," she said, and that struck him as funny. Like, be careful and don't die of cancer on the way home?

"I will," he said, which was simpler. "Bye, Molly. It was good to see you."

At home, Dora came out of the building as he stepped from the cab. He suspected she had been watching for him, but she held up a trash bag as proof that she had a very good reason to be there at that time. "You are good?" she asked him, and walked back with him into the building.

He shrugged.

"So, you're not good, then?"

"Well, I'm not dead," he said, and she smiled and patted his arm.

"Then you are good," she told him.

4.

The second time Steven found out he was dying was a lot like the first. The doctor—this one a woman, and older—was sympathetic, even apologetic as she delivered the news that Steven already knew: the cancer had returned. That sounded wrong to him, so he interrupted her practiced deliverance of the diagnosis and his options.

"Only it never left," he said, "so how can it return?"

She stopped in mid-sentence, her mouth agape, her eyes wide. "I'm sorry?"

"You said the cancer had returned," he said, "and I said that was wrong, because it had never really gone away. It was still there." And he pointed to his scar, where it crested just slightly behind his temple. "The radiation and the chemo kept it under control, and that worked for five whole years, but it's growing again." He paused. "So, it hasn't returned. It just never left."

The doctor nodded. "Right. Yes. You're absolutely right. So, let's examine your options…"

Nothing had changed: he could have the surgery and begin a regimen of radiation as soon as was medically possible, followed by chemotherapy. It was, same as last time, his only hope for survival, and even if he did "survive," he only had a maximum of three years left to live. He had already lived five since his last diagnosis.

"What if I didn't have the surgery?" he asked.

The doctor's face registered her disbelief. "Well... that would be a very unorthodox approach to treatment," she managed to say.

Steven chuckled. "I didn't mean *never* have the surgery. I meant right now. What if we did radiation and chemo first, then surgery?" It occurred to him as he said it that he had done just that, and still here he was. "I mean... is there something different we can do? Something new?"

"I could put you in touch with a service that could match you with a clinical trial," she said, "but there are no guarantees you would meet all the criteria."

He nodded. "Okay." He really didn't want to have this surgery again. The recovery had been torturous the last time, and by the time he had started feeling better, he'd begun the radiation treatments. Then the chemotherapy. He couldn't remember the last time he had felt good, free of pain, no headaches or pressure behind his eyes, or nausea. He just wanted to have a good day again. An actual, *real* good day, not one where he just told people he was feeling good to avoid their sympathy and questions.

"If I may say, I think surgery first, followed by the radiation, followed by the chemotherapy is your best option," she told him.

"Can I think about it for a day or two?" he asked.

The doctor was completely nonplussed. "Yes. Yes, of course."

At home, Dora was sweeping the steps of the building. She frowned when she saw the look on his face. "What is this face?" she asked, and gestured at it with the handle of her broom. "You look like someone is stealing your candy."

He gave her a weak smile. "The cancer," he said. "It's back."

"But when did it leave?"

That made him laugh. "See, that's what I said!" He sat on the front stoop and she sat with him and they were silent for a moment.

"So what will you do?" she asked.

Steven shrugged. "If I have the surgery, the cancer doesn't go away," he said, to their feet. "If I don't have the surgery, the cancer doesn't go away." Another shrug. "Either way, I die in the end."

"Bah!" she said, and swiped at the air with both her arms, like she meant to scoop it up and carry it some place, or dump it on him. "Crazy talk! Who says you die?"

"Um... the cancer?"

"Bah!" Again with the swiping of the air. "They told me I should die once, too, and I thought I would." She held up a finger. "But then I didn't." And she pointed to the tattoo on her left forearm, the numbers smudged by the years but still as legible as the day they were scrawled onto her arm. "Then I was supposed to die again and I didn't. A thousand times I should have died and a thousand times I didn't. That was their truth, not mine." She shook her head vehemently and glared at a spot somewhere in front of her.

Steven felt like a fool, and though he knew a glioblastoma and surviving Auschwitz were two very different things, he didn't want to be impertinent, so he stayed silent.

"Who says you have to die?" she asked him again, now looking at him hard.

"Well... this form of cancer is aggressive, and—"

She cut him short. "But you had this surgery before, then you had the radiation and the chemotherapy, and you lived," she pointed out.

"Well, yes..."

"They told you three years." She held up three fingers, the knuckles swollen with arthritis. "But here you are still. You should be dead now. For two years you should be dead. So why not?"

Steven opened his mouth, then closed it again, several times in a row. He was sure he looked a lot like a fish, but he couldn't find the right words to express what he wanted to say. "I don't know," he said, at last.

"And they don't, either, all these doctors." She stabbed at the air between them with one finger. "They guess, and maybe they get it right and maybe they don't. You want to live?" Steven opened his mouth to answer the question, but she didn't wait for him. "Then you live," she told him, with finality. "You find a reason, and you live for it. I know this because I did it. I should have been dead seventy years ago, but here I am. Still living." She stood with some difficulty, using Steven's shoulder for support. "I'm going to eat now, you want some? I made borscht."

"Sounds good," he said, and stood to hold the door for her.

Neither of them noticed the man who had parked across the street until he reached the steps to their building and spoke just before they stepped inside. "Steven?"

They both turned at the voice, and Steven actually gasped. "Kevin? What are you doing here?"

"You know him?" Dora asked over his shoulder.

"Yeah. He used to be my boyfriend."

They had lived together for five years. Janine had introduced them, convinced of their compatibility. "You both like all the same things, and you act alike, and you even *look* alike, for shit's sake," had been her rationale. "If this isn't meant to be, then I don't know what is."

She was right, too, for the most part. Neither thought they looked much alike: Steven was short and slight and more olive-complexioned where Kevin was taller, broader, more solid. "Big boned," Kevin called it, and they laughed. Steven's nose was bigger; Kevin's ears stuck out. But they did share an enthusiasm for many of the same things—old horror films, classic television shows, junk food.

They had sex on the first date. Furtive, ungraceful sex that had them chuckling about it afterward. "Now we have to see each other again," Kevin reasoned. "I can't let you think I'm always that awkward in bed."

So, they dated. Then they got an apartment together. Janine gloried in the success of their relationship. "I'm such a yenta!" she declared many times, and Steven just rolled his eyes.

That was six years ago. Kevin had come to him and announced his intent to move west with his job. He'd wanted Steven to come, too. Steven had actually said he needed to think about it, but he knew he wasn't going to move to California, he just didn't know why he didn't want to go. Then, so he would not have to fabricate a reason, he cheated on Kevin and that made it easier. They broke their lease and Kevin moved west and Steven moved into the apartment he was living in now, the one upstairs from Dora Zitler.

A year later, give or take, he received his diagnosis. He suspected the two were somehow connected, he just couldn't prove it scientifically, so he kept the theory to himself.

"Are you back?" he asked.

"Just visiting," Kevin told him. "My mom still lives in Alpharetta."

"Oh."

They sat on the steps, Dora gone to tend to her borscht. The silence was awkward. Steven's mind spun with all the things he might say—how was California? how was work? were the earthquakes as terrifying as he always imagined they were? was Kevin seeing anyone?—but never settled on anything, so he popped his knuckles and stared at a line of ants passing by on the sidewalk an inch or so from his shoe.

"I ran into Janine and she gave me your address," Kevin said. "I hope that's okay."

Steven shrugged. "It's fine."

"And she told me about your... the diagnosis, too." A pause. "That really fucking sucks. I don't know what else to say."

Steven gave another shrug. "There's not really anything to say, I guess. I drew the short straw." Even as he said it, he knew it sounded like self-pity and he hated himself for it, but he couldn't take it back.

"What's the prognosis?" Kevin seemed genuinely interested.

"Well, I was supposed to be dead already, according to the first doctor, so who knows at this point?"

Kevin placed a hand on Steven's knee, and it was just as big and soft and warm as Steven remembered. "I'm sorry," he said, simply, and that made Steven break down for the first time in years. Kevin slipped an arm around him and pulled him close and let him cry.

Later they lay together on Steven's bed, their shoes scattered on the floor. Kevin flexed his toes and they popped. Steven still couldn't settle on any one thing he wanted to say, and he wanted to make sure that when he did say something that it was what needed to be said, so instead of speaking, he just lay there and stared at the ceiling.

"Janine told me about the baby thing," Kevin said. "That's really cool."

Steven was confused. He propped himself up on his elbows and stared at Kevin. "What baby thing?" If Janine was pregnant, she hadn't told him.

"The donation thing?" Kevin said. "She and Molly having a baby, and you being the donor...?" He realized his error and his cheeks flushed pink, the way Steven remembered. "Oh. Maybe I got it wrong."

"They want me to be the father of their baby?" Speaking it aloud helped Steven to understand it. "They haven't asked me about it." Or perhaps they had and he'd just forgotten. Only he didn't have those memory lapses anymore the way he'd had immediately following the surgery, so it was doubtful that the three of them had such a conversation and he had simply forgotten. He would certainly remember being asked to father a child.

"I might have misunderstood," Kevin said, also raising up on his elbows. "Don't let it worry you. You have more important things to worry about right now."

Steven wanted to kiss him, and he made a move to do just that, but stopped himself. If Kevin noticed it, he didn't remark on it.

"I don't *think* they asked me," he said. "I forget things sometimes."

Kevin reached over and rubbed what remained of his hair. "Don't worry about it. And if they bring it up, remember to act surprised. I'd hate to think I ruined the surprise."

They lay back again and another awkward silence ensued. Steven thought of Dora and her borscht, and the tattoo on her forearm and how it was still as blue now as the day she received it, though the numbers themselves weren't so easily deciphered. What must it have been like to wake every morning and wonder if you'd live through the day, and not because of cancer or a brain tumor. He knew he was far from knocking on death's door. When he woke every day, he ran through a regimen of tests of all his motor functions: he flexed his fingers and toes, he lifted his legs, he sat up and lay back down; he spoke his name, then his Hebrew name, then the day of the week and the date; he stood and walked around the bed, he tested his depth perception, his vision, his reading. Dora had awakened every day in Auschwitz capable of all those things, surely, but still with no guarantee that she would live or die. He felt discomfited as he recalled their talk on the steps when Dora had scolded him for practically giving up. He needed to find a reason to live, like she'd said. Something more meaningful than the simple desire not to die.

"So, I should go," Kevin said and sat up.

It disappointed Steven more than he dared to admit. "How long are you in town?"

"Until Sunday." Kevin found his shoes and stuffed his feet into them. Vans slip-ons, which were his preference.

What Steven wanted to say was how much he longed to see Kevin again, and to apologize, because he never had before, and he may not get too many other chances to do so, with Kevin living on the other side of the country. He wanted to make Kevin—this big, gentle St. Bernard of a guy—understand once and for all that the reason Steven had fucked around on him had nothing to do with Kevin and everything to do with himself, make him understand that people like Steven don't do the things they do to hurt the people around them, no; they do it to hurt themselves, because that is what having a self-destructive personality is all about. And that when you live your entire life trying to degrade yourself and nothing ever seems to really stick, it is only the most profound universal justice imaginable that you would end up with some inoperable something, because that's what you deserve. It's what you've really wanted your entire life.

That's what he wanted to say, but all he could really manage was "Well, maybe I'll see you again."

And Kevin smiled, and there were his dimples, and they almost broke Steven's heart. "I'd like that," he said.

Dora had questions, and they sat at her table in her cluttered apartment, bowls of borscht between them. "It was a long time ago with this boy?" she asked him.

Steven nodded. "Before I moved here."

"You were together long?"

"Five years."

Her eyes widened and her head inclined toward him, a look of confusion. Or maybe she was telling him to go ahead, explain, and so he did.

"We were young," he told her, around a mouthful of soup. "We were introduced by a mutual friend, and when you're young and stupid you do stupid things, and in less than a month we were living together." He shrugged. "And we lived together for the next five years. He got a job in California, and he really wanted to go there, but I didn't." Another shrug. "So, we broke up. He moved to California and I stayed here."

"Oh," she said, but she did not sound satisfied with that explanation.

"Today was the first time I've seen him in five years."

Dora nodded.

Her scrutiny was making him uncomfortable. He could either sit and eat his soup, or he could escape her gaze, but he couldn't manage both at the same time, so he chose to change the subject. "How long were you and your husband married?"

"A long time," she said, and pushed a chunk of beet around her bowl with her spoon. Then: "What is his name, this boy?"

He shot her a look. "Kevin."

"He's Jewish?" Dora was really starting to sound like a grandmother.

Steven shrugged. "He isn't much of anything, really. Or, rather, he wasn't then."

Dora scowled. "You're born Jewish, you don't get to opt out. You either are or you're not."

That made him chuckle. "Then, yes. He's Jewish."

She nodded. "He looks Jewish."

"So, what? You're saying you approve of him?"

Dora gave a theatrical shrug. "How can I know this if I don't know him? I only know what you tell me. I know his name. He lives in California. He's Jewish. What else do I need to know about this boy?"

His own mother had not taken such an interest in Kevin. "Nothing," Steven told her. "You don't need to know anything. You'll never see him again, anyway. He's only here through Sunday."

"I see," she said. "In that case, why was he here?"

"He heard about the cancer…"

"And what? He comes to heal you? He's a doctor, this boy?"

Steven rolled his eyes. "No. Stop being such a yenta. He's not a doctor."

"I'm just trying to understand why he drives all the way from California to see you because of your cancer, but you broke up five years ago and you haven't spoken since." More of the dramatic shrugging, like she was on a stage and needed to make certain the people in the cheap seats could read her body language.

He sighed. "His mom lives in Alpharetta, and he ran into Janine. She told him about the cancer, and she gave him my address." It occurred to him then that she could have just given Kevin his phone number instead of his address, and suddenly it seemed a bit odd to her, too. Maybe Kevin was up to something. And maybe Janine was in on it.

"Oh," was all Dora said.

"And anyway, we're not getting back together, if that's what you're thinking," Steven continued. His borscht was starting to get cold. "He's just a really nice guy, and that's the kind of shit he does." He couldn't decide if the exasperation he was suddenly feeling was because of Kevin, or Dora, or himself. "He'll probably call once a week when he gets back to San Francisco, to see how I'm doing, and he'll call once a week until I'm dead." He paused for emphasis. "Then he'll want to help plan the funeral, and he'll cook all the food for the shivah, and he'll clean the house, and he'll visit the grave every month until he can't walk anymore. Hell, he'll even visit your grave, Dora, because *that's the kind of shit he does.*" His arms were spread wide, like Dora's exaggerated shrugs, like they were performing this and the things they did with their arms were as much a part of the scene as what came out of their mouths.

"He sounds like a good boy," Dora said.

Steven made a noise that was neither agreement nor dispute.

"Who in their right mind lets a boy like this get away?"

And one of those smiles that people give when they've been caught at something spread across his face. He couldn't help it. "See, that's the funny part," he said. "I didn't let him get away. I ran him off."

"Bah!" Dora swatted at the air like she had earlier. "This is crazy talk!"

"It may be. But it's the truth. I cheated on him and he left." It was his turn to give her a stage-perfect shrug.

She gaped at him across the table and her eyes flickered to his half-eaten bowl of borscht. "You want some more?"

The retelling of it made it sound simple, like Steven had just one day decided that it was time for him to look for sex outside his relationship, so he had chosen some guy at random, done it, then went home and told Kevin that he'd done it, and Kevin had stormed out in a rage. The way it happened in movies, where everything went from good to bad to something tolerable in two hours or less. But it actually took four of the five years they were together, and it really only came down to one thing: Steven had gotten bored. He suspected the results would be the same were he to give it another shot.

5.

Janine and Molly invited him for dinner and he considered calling back to cancel. He even practiced excuses as he decided what to wear, as he showered, as he brushed his teeth. "I'm just really exhausted lately." But he'd worked all day, so he doubted that would be believable. "I just started a new medication." Only he hadn't; in fact he'd told Janine just last week that he was having fewer headaches and dizziness, so he was relying less on pills. He was in the cab and halfway across town when he thought he might just turn around and go back home and just tell Janine, when she asked, that he'd totally forgotten. He'd had a tumor removed from his brain, after all. Surely it was plausible.

"Here you go, my friend," the driver told him then, and repeated back Janine and Molly's address for him.

Steven laughed. "Guess I can't back out now," he muttered.

"Excuse me?" the driver asked.

"Nothing." Steven paid him and got out.

Molly answered the door when he rang. "Your hair!" was the first thing she said, then she hugged him. It had been several months since she'd seen him, and his hair was almost as thick and curly as it had been before he started the chemo and radiation.

"Yeah," he said, and rubbed his scar. It comforted him, for some reason he couldn't adequately explain, and had become his newest habit.

Janine was in the kitchen. She insisted on hugging him, though they'd seen one another the day before at work. She had made spaghetti, and there was wine. Steven found it increasingly difficult to pretend he didn't know why they had invited him over.

He had texted Kevin earlier. *I think they're going to pop the question tonight.*

From Kevin: *Did you decide yes or no?*

Not yet, he responded. *It's still so weird.*

"You look amazing," Molly said once they were seated. "You look really healthy. And your hair is coming back."

"Thanks," Steven said, because he wasn't sure what else you were supposed to say when someone told you that you didn't look like you were dying anymore.

"And you're putting your weight back on," Janine pointed out.

"Are you saying I'm fat?"

They laughed. Janine and Molly exchanged glances across the table and Steven pretended he didn't notice. Janine said, "So, dinner wasn't the only reason we asked you over tonight, Steven."

He very nearly replied that he already knew, but Molly cut him short. "But we can talk about that after we eat," she said, and gave Janine a very pointed look.

Janine rolled her eyes. "Yeah, okay. Whatever."

Later, they sat on the floor and Janine poured them more wine. Steven gulped his.

"So, Steven, you know Janine and I have been together for a while now," Molly began. He glanced from one to the other and back again. He imagined he looked like a cartoon character watching a game of tennis.

"Twelve years," Janine said.

"Thirteen," Molly corrected her, and Janine threw her a look. "It will be thirteen years in five months, so why not just say thirteen?"

Janine rolled her eyes again and Steven drank more wine. The last thing he wanted was to get in the middle of one of their spats. Janine and Molly never really fought, they just went back and forth like this— one of them said something and the other corrected her, then the first explained why she saw it the way she did, and the second explained her perspective, which lead to further disagreement and just hearing it and watching it was exhausting. Steven couldn't imagine being one of the participants in such an exchange. He took another gulp of wine and interrupted them. "You guys want me to father a child for you."

They both stopped in mid-sentence, mouths and eyes wide with surprise.

"Kevin told me," he explained. To Janine: "He said you mentioned you had asked me, or were going to ask me. He couldn't remember exactly, but he told me to act surprised when you guys did finally ask me, so..." His voice trailed off.

Janine raked her fingers through her hair, actually tugged at the spikiness of it. Molly sat and nodded, over and over, just nodded.

"I guess this is me being surprised," Steven added at last. "That you would even ask me to begin with." He paused, thinking. "Actually, I'm surprised that you guys want to have a baby. Where the hell did that come from?"

They explained and he listened. Janine spoke of biological clocks, Mother Nature, destiny; Molly seemed to give a lecture on how the female reproductive system worked. Steven found it difficult to follow after a few minutes and felt himself zoning out, coming up with excuses to leave. He blamed the wine. He had still not worked back up to his pre-cancer level of consumption.

"And... that's it, really," Janine said, after what seemed an eternity.

Molly nodded. "Yeah," she agreed. "I mean, when we made a list of all the men we knew—gay or straight—you were really the only one that checked off all the boxes."

"Thanks, I guess," Steven said, and when he laughed he sounded nervous.

"Seriously, Steven. You're smart, you're witty... you're good-looking." Janine counted his qualities on her fingers. "You have good hair."

"And cancer," he pointed out, raising a finger of his own.

She fell silent then, traded a look with Molly.

"I mean... what if this is genetic? Like, what if I was born with this, and it's been lying there, waiting for just the right moment in my life... the right conditions? What if I father a child for you and... and this happens?" He pointed to his head for emphasis. "Like... how do we know it won't happen?" It really hadn't occurred to him, really, until he said it, and hearing the words come out of his mouth made it real, urgent.

Janine and Molly sat there, holding hands, silent. They probably hadn't planned on this response from him. Or maybe they had and just hadn't discussed their own response to it.

"Because that would suck," he said after a moment, breaking the silence.

Janine nodded. "Yeah, that would suck," she said, then asked, "Did your mother know when you were born that when you were thirty years old you'd develop a brain tumor?" When Steven didn't reply, she turned to Molly, then back to him. "I think it's a risk we're prepared to take, Steven."

He stared at the dregs of the wine in his glass. In seconds, he saw this life of this unborn child—this child that hadn't even been conceived—flash before his eyes: screaming at birth, nursing, having his diaper changed (for some reason, he pictured a boy), then pre-school and kindergarten, and Janine and Molly in tears as he walked away from them into his new classroom where a pretty, young teacher waited. He realized the boy looked a lot like him at that age, but he allowed the vision to run its course, through

263

elementary school and into high school, beyond pubescent awkwardness and on to college, to travel the world, to fall in love. And this child who didn't exist yet met a guy and fell in love and that guy looked a lot like Kevin, and even when Steven tried to insert a brain tumor into the scenario, the vision resisted and the child he might father continued on, had children of his own and dogs, and walked on a beach with his family.

"Well?" Molly asked, and it broke his reverie.

Steven breathed an enormous sigh. "I don't know," he said. "Can I think about it?"

Janine and Molly laughed. "Of course, silly," Janine said, and slapped him on the arm. "We didn't expect an answer tonight. Take all the time you need."

Steven nodded, and that voice in the back of his head was there to remind him that he didn't exactly have all the time in the world.

And he did think about it. On the cab ride home, then as he tried to fall to sleep, then all day at work the next day as he sucked down cup after cup of coffee to stay awake. He caught Janine eyeing him at intervals and when she approached, he pretended to be too involved in something—organizing beneath the information counter, searching for something on the computer—to talk. She didn't pressure him, though, and for that he was glad.

Steven wanted to talk to Dora about it more than anyone. Not that he needed her advice, because she'd probably just throw his dilemma back at him the way she always did. It occurred to him that her habit of listening, only to hand him his problem back to him for him to solve was probably the reason he felt such a need to talk to her about this new thing that had presented itself.

When he knocked at Dora's, there was no answer, which he found odd. He turned the knob and found the door locked, which was doubly odd. A tiny flare of panic erupted in his gut and he dialed her number, heard it ring from inside her empty apartment. By the time he hung up, his panic was full-blown and he felt a panic attack forming somewhere in the space between his chest and his brain.

Steven imagined the worst possible scenarios: Dora had fallen and dislocated her hip and been hospitalized, which was both good and bad at that age, because it was usually a rapid decline in the wake of a hip injury like that; or she had hit her head and was comatose and might never revive; she had gone out to the Indian market two blocks over and been mugged and was now bleeding to death on the sidewalk while uncaring passersby stepped over her.

He considered calling all the hospitals, but abandoned that idea when he realized there were too many hospitals in the city, and if Dora was lying in one of them, dying, she would probably be dead by the time he contacted the right one; then he would be told nothing because he was not actually next of kin. He thought he might call the police—didn't they keep a log of emergency calls? But his hand shook violently as he tried to search for the number to the nearest precinct, so he just ended up calling Kevin.

"Calm down," Kevin said, and his voice was like caramel. "I'm sure she's just fine."

"But she's always at home," Steven pointed out. "I mean, like, I don't even know how she has food, because I never see her leave or come back from anywhere." He laughed as he realized what he'd just said.

"Maybe she has her groceries delivered," Kevin suggested.

"Maybe. But, whatever, because she's not at home right now and that can't be good, and I don't know where she is and I don't know what to do."

"Maybe she's visiting her family."

Steven opened his mouth to protest further: she didn't have a family, her husband had died years ago, she didn't have any children, and anyone else that hadn't survived the Holocaust had passed away. But it only took him a second to realize that the only thing he did know for certain was that Dora's husband had died; he had just assumed the rest.

"Maybe..."

"Don't worry about it, Steven. You've got enough to worry about. If you don't hear from her in a couple days, *then* you can start worrying."

Steven's mind spun with all manner of scenarios. Dora, lying unconscious in her apartment while he worried about himself instead was the vision that came most to his mind. He shook it off and it immediately returned.

"I'll be there next weekend," Kevin said. "I'd like to see you."

"Yes," Steven heard himself say, but his mind was two days into the future, calling the police to report a missing person. "I'd like that, too."

Kevin was right.

Dora returned the next day, a Thursday, her insistent knocking rousing Steven from a fitful nap on the sofa. He was only partially awake when he opened the door and she practically threw herself at him, gripped his arm, her eyes wide. "Oh! Thank goodness you are here," she panted, slightly out of breath. "Thank goodness you are well."

"I'm good," he said. "Where have you been?"

"This is why I am here," she said.

"I was worried sick..."

"For this, I am so sorry. I have been with my daughter and her family." And she proceeded to explain that she'd written a note, then left it in her apartment and by the time she realized it, she was on her way to her daughter's. And she didn't have his number memorized, not like she used to memorize people's numbers; she only hit the number two on her phone and it dialed his number. "And when I call information, I am told they can not look up your mobile phone number." She waved her arms, like she was fighting progress.

"I told her not to worry about it," said a woman behind Dora, who Steven immediately knew to be her daughter. They were identical, only the daughter was younger, slightly taller, and did not bother to dye her hair. "She wouldn't be gone for long, just a couple days."

"It is the yahrzeit of my husband," Dora explained, but she never let go of Steven's arm.

"Well, I'm relieved to know you're okay," he said, and decided not to share all the horrible visions he'd had while she was away.

"Let's go, Mama," said the daughter, and pulled on the arm Dora did not have attached to Steven. "We need to get you unpacked and settled in."

But Dora would not let go of Steven's arm. "You are not mad at me?" she asked, her eyes beseeching.

He smiled. "No. I'm not mad."

Dora smiled, too. "This is good." Only then would she allow her daughter to lead her away.

When he told her about the decision he had to make, they were sitting outside in the courtyard of the building. All the units opened onto it or overlooked it, but only Dora took it upon herself to plant things and tend them. There were ferns and hostas and Japanese maples; in the spring there would be tulips and daffodils, and in the summer, gladiolus. The management didn't seem to mind, and they could charge people more because of its lushness.

Dora sat and nursed a cup of coffee while Steven pulled weeds and trimmed rosemary and snipped dead leaves from the camellia, which would be bright pink when it bloomed. The weather was unusually hot for late October, but Dora had wrapped herself in a thick shawl.

"Careful," she said to him. "If you trim down too much, this will kill the rosemary."

"I'm being careful," he said. He doubted anything he might do would kill the damned thing anyway. It thrived in the shade, without water or rain for extended periods, and was slowly becoming a tree. It occurred to him that the rosemary was a lot like him, or he it: it took a lot to kill it.

"You have heard again from this boy?" Dora called to him.

"Yes."

She grinned. "And?"

"He's coming in next weekend."

"I'll make a brisket!"

"You don't have to do that," he said, and stood, a clump of weeds in one hand. His equilibrium was still slightly off, probably always would be, so he steadied himself against the table where she sat.

Dora swiped at the air. "It's brisket," she said. "You put it in the oven and it cooks. I'm not killing the cow."

Steven sat across from her. "Why don't I cook for a change?"

Her eyes widened. "You cook?"

The remark won her a look of disdain. "Yes, I cook."

Dora shrugged. "Who am I to turn down an invitation to dinner when someone else wants to cook?"

They lapsed into silence. Steven inspected the stains on the tips of his fingers from the weeds he'd pulled. He smelled the greenness and that familiar bloom of dread opened in his chest. He thought *I wonder how much more time I have to smell those weeds, to sit here with Dora, feel the sun on my ears...* He felt the color drain from his face but could think of nothing he might do to make it less obvious. His heart pounded in his chest and he tried to breathe through his nose to quiet it. He had never had an anxiety attack in front of Dora, and he did not want to start now.

Dora regarded him over her cup. If she noticed anything, she did not give anything away with her expression. "This boy," she said, and set her cup down so softly it did not make a sound as it came in contact with the saucer. "This Kevin."

"What about him?" Steven asked.

"I think this is good that he is coming. I think maybe you should think of being with him again." And she paused to give one of her dramatic shrugs. "I am not so young anymore. Maybe I will not always be here, and then who will you have?"

It occurred to Steven that he would probably go before Dora did, but he did not say that. Instead he asked, "And what brings this up, all of a sudden?"

She shrugged again and looked down into her cup. She would not meet his eyes. After a long moment, she spoke. "Years ago—you would have been very little, this was when Ronald Reagan was President—there was a group of us, a great many people, and we got together once a year. A—what is this word?" She tapped her forehead lightly, as if that might dislodge the word she sought.

"A convention?" Steven asked.

"Yes," she said. "Thank you. Yes. A *convention,* you know, but smaller. A couple hundred people. All survivors of the Holocaust. And we got together once a year, and you know what we talked about?" Now she met his eyes.

Steven shrugged. "The concentration camps?"

Dora shook her head. "We traded recipes, and we talked about our children, and grandchildren, and where we went for vacation that year, and the books we read, and the movies we saw." She stared into her cup. "We talked about anything but the Holocaust. Because, you see, it was very important for us to be just like everyone else, not always the poor victims, the poor survivors of the Holocaust. Even though we were together with the only other people who would understand, and who we could speak to about the camps and the death marches... we traded recipes and talked about the soap operas." She waved her hand, not dismissing the subject, but perhaps just sliding it to the side. "And when we weren't together, we wrote letters. This was when people actually wrote letters, with a pen and paper. And we sent cards and photographs and patterns for knitting and sewing." She waved her hands as if to say *everything... we shared everything*.

"That must have been nice," Steven said, unsure of where she was going, but glad for her doing all the talking because it allowed him to settle his breathing and calm his nerves. The dread was still there, but it had grown smaller, the way it always did.

Dora gave a small, noncommittal shrug.

"Do you still keep in touch?" he asked.

"This is just it, though," she said. "Every year, there are less of us. I made so many friends this way—Etty, Hertha, Chaim, Otto... and every year, we go to this gathering of the survivors." The look on her face changed as she focused on a spot just beyond Steven, where he sat. "Then one year, not really so long ago, maybe fifteen years ago... I am preparing to go, and the phone rings and it is my friend Morris, and he tells me he will not see me that year, but he wanted to call me so that he could hear my voice and wish me a happy birthday." She focused her eyes on Steven and added, almost as an aside, "My birthday always fell the week after these gatherings." Then she picked up the thread of her narrative. "Anyway, I go and Morris is not there, and the next thing I know, I am receiving a letter from his son. Morris has died, this letter tells me."

"Were you close?" Steven heard himself ask. He'd never realized how generic a question it was until he heard himself ask it then.

"We saw each other once a year," she said. "Other than that, it was cards and letters. Sometimes a call on the phone. He was older than I was, his wife had died some while ago. We were both at Auschwitz together, though we didn't know this until later." She picked up her coffee, took a drink, made a face. "Bah. That's cold."

"You want me to make you some more?" Steven asked.

"Not right now," she told him. "I want to finish what I am telling you. Then we can make more coffee."

A slightly different form of dread settled onto Steven's chest then, and he suddenly didn't want Dora to finish her reminiscence. He just couldn't think of the best way to communicate that to her. "Okay...," he said instead.

She nodded. "Anyway, like I say. Morris. He dies. The next year, someone else. People I know, people I don't know, it doesn't matter. Every year I go, and every year, there are fewer and fewer of us alive to be there. First it is Morris... then it is Hertha... then Otto and Chaim and Etty, all in the same year, and every time, I get a letter or I get a phone call. Somebody's always saying goodbye." She sighed. "It is like this, getting old. These days, I don't think we have the survivors getting together like before. There are not that many of us, and we are all so old now. Or there are the children who survived, but they have no memory of what happened, really, only what they have been told."

Steven waited for her to continue, or say something that made it clear she had said all she wanted to say. Even though he dreaded what she was getting at, he waited for it, staring down at his hands in his lap, or the clump of dead weeds on top of the table, or Dora's cup of cold coffee. He guessed he would outlive everyone. At some point that would have to be a record, wouldn't it? A man was given three years to live on two separate occasions, but he lived. He kept living and he had to watch everyone around him go before him: his dad, now Dora, and next, he guessed, would be his mother.

"Anyway," Dora finally said. "Bah! I am talking like an old woman." She stood, took her cup and flung the cold coffee from it into the bushes Steven had so meticulously weeded. "Let's go inside."

Steven had felt himself on the verge of tears, but now he laughed. "What?"

Dora turned back to him. "What do you mean *what?*"

He still sat, pointed at her empty chair. "You just sat there and told me you were dying, and you're

274

just going to leave it there, and let's go inside? And make coffee?"

The woman's face was a caricature of confusion. "What? I did not say this."

And Steven realized she was right, Dora hadn't actually said "I am dying," but she'd said everything but. "Then what was that all about?" he asked, gesticulating wildly: at Dora, at her chair, at her coffee cup, at the insanity of everything.

Dora shrugged. "This is what I am thinking," she said, simply, "so I tell you. You think I am telling you I'm *dying?* No! I am just... missing them, all my friends who are gone. The way I will miss you when you are gone. This is why I am thinking of them now, because I am thinking of what it will be like here when you are not here."

Steven bent forward with his head between his knees and felt the blood vessels behind his eyes fill with blood. When his ears started to pound, he put his hands over them and just listened to the sound, like an electronic simulation of an ocean. It took a minute to realize he was laughing, then another minute to understand it was with relief. For a solid five minutes, he had prepared himself to hear the worst from Dora—she was dying; whatever the circumstance, be it old age or some newly manifested condition, she would not be around much longer; she was old and it was her time—only to have her do a complete one-eighty. He felt giddy with relief.

"Are you okay?" he heard Dora ask through the blood pounding in his ears.

"Yes," he said, still laughing. "Yes. I'm perfectly fine. I thought you were dying, but you're not, and Janine and Molly asked me to father a child with them." Just like that, in one breath, he told her.

For a moment, he stood there, straddling confusion that he had understood her to say she was dying, and surprise at the last thing he'd said. Dora's eyes widened. "A baby?"

Steven nodded. He sat up finally, and as the blood returned to all the other parts of his body, he felt exhausted. "Yeah," he said. "Crazy, isn't it? And it suddenly makes sense why they want me to be the one."

Dora cocked her head at him. "And why is this?"

"Because it will be better for them to have a child that they don't have to share with someone else," he said. He had never thought that before, but as he sat and felt the blood drain from his head, it came to him the way the solutions to complex math problems had come to him in college: so unexpectedly and clearly that it shamed him to think he hadn't seen it sooner.

She frowned, glanced down at the empty coffee cup she held in her hand, then back at Steven.

He stood. "Let's go inside. You need coffee and I think I may need to take something for my head."

6.

"How are you feeling?" Kevin asked him when he called.

"Fine," Steven said, though that wasn't really true. He did feel fine, but he couldn't shake the suspicion that something was wrong, like the cancer was playing tricks with him, pretending to be gone but really only hiding out somewhere the CAT scans and MRIs couldn't reach. He was lying on his bed, on top of the blanket in socks and underwear, the way he did as a child. His window was open and he could hear someone's dog barking, a siren in the distance, voices closer arguing. He closed his eyes and pictured his tumor hiding in a tree while a dog barked up at it from the ground.

"That's good!" There was real joy in Kevin's voice when he said it.

"Yeah, it is," Steven said. "I have my next follow-up on Thursday."

"You can tell me all about it when I get in on Friday," Kevin said.

That reminded Steven, and he said, "I'm giving Janine and Molly my decision on Friday, too," he said.

"Oh?" A pause. "What are you going to tell them?"

"I haven't decided," Steven said, and that made Kevin laugh.

"Well, how can you give them your decision if you haven't made it?" he asked.

Steven chuckled, too. "I don't know. I set that date for myself, hoping a deadline would light a fire under me, but I can't really decide. I'm still going back and forth, and I don't really know why."

"Well, it's a big decision," Kevin said.

"Yeah," Steven replied. *But not really,* he thought. Really all he needed to do was jack off into a cup and his role was done. Well, blood tests and an HIV screening before, but he knew what the results of all those would be; and he masturbated regularly, so that wasn't the hindrance. He just really couldn't put his finger on why he was dragging his heels on this. "I should just tell Janine tomorrow that I'll do it," he said, thinking out loud.

He could actually hear Kevin considering that on the other end. "What's stopping you?"

"I don't know..."

"Okay," he told Janine the next day. They were alone in the break room, and he was pretending to read a magazine while she pretended not to want to ask him if he'd reached a decision.

She stopped chewing her banana and looked up, feigning mild confusion. "Okay?"

Steven nodded. "Yes. I'm saying yes." Then he watched as her face went through a range of emotions, like a Doppler radar weather map: first, relief, then surprise moved in from the west, followed by partial happiness, then tears. He stayed where he sat though it felt awkward. He didn't know what to say, so he said nothing and waited for Janine to get her emotions under control.

"I've got to call Molly!"

"Of course," Steven said.

He'd expected her to leave the room to make the call, but she took out her phone and called Molly right there in front of him. "He said yes," Janine shouted into the phone. "He said yes! Oh my God!" And she leaned back in her chair, like she might faint. Steven hoped that didn't happen, since he had no idea what should be done if someone fainted.

Through the phone, he could hear Molly screaming. Janine said, "Oh my God! Oh my God!" Over and over, and it struck Steven as odd, because she always claimed she was atheist.

"What did you tell Janine?" Kevin asked him on Friday.

They'd had sex and Steven was actually struck by how comfortable it had been, like they hadn't been apart for as long as they'd been and noting had ever gone wrong. He was on his side with his head against Kevin's shoulder. The smell of Kevin was so familiar when he breathed, like grass almost.

"I told her yes," Steven said.

Kevin's big arm slipped around him and squeezed him gently in a half hug. "That was a good thing you did," he said.

Steven could think of no appropriate reply, so he said nothing. Instead, he was gripped again by that vision of the future of which he was no part: Janine and Molly at the reproductive health clinic for the procedure, nervous for the first visit, but rejoicing when told it's successful; Janine and Molly after the delivery of their child, a son (it is always a boy); Janine and Molly waking up at all hours of the night, first one and then the other. He imagined the child's first words, his first steps, and then, later, riding a bike, skateboarding, playing sports. He saw Janine and Molly tearful on the boy's first day of school, then the last day of school, then the last day of college. The boy still looked a lot like him, and he didn't try to change that in his mind, he just let it go as it would, and never once did the shadow of cancer spring up or lurk in the shadows.

Acknowledgements

Thanks to Rebecca Weisberg for reading and being honest... and thanks to Debra Ginsberg, just because.

85957599R00156

Made in the USA
Lexington, KY
06 April 2018